TONI J. WALKER

I0628234

Saints, Ain'ts, and Sistahs
A Novel by Toni J. Walker

The original version of this book was titled "The
Sistahhood Pact" and was written in 2008. The
name has been changed, and the original version
was not released.

All Scripture quotations, unless otherwise indicated,
are taken from the Holy Bible.

ISBN: 978-1-7346583-0-9
Copyright © 2022 by Toni J. Walker
Cover Image Credit: Toni J. Walker
U.S. Price $14.95
Published in the United States of America.

SAINTS. AIN'TS, AND SISTAHS

ACKNOWLEGEMENTS

First of all, giving acknowledgement and glory to God.

To my mother, Ruth Dixon, also known as Ms. Walker, I wish you were here so we could read this together and laugh.

To my sister, Trina Fosha, I wish you were here. I miss you so much.

To Cookie Johnson and Lon Rosen. OMG, words cannot express my appreciation.

To those of you who read the novel and suffered through my numerous, undecided book covers, Marie Terrell, Rihana Acklin, Dorothy Scott, Tyra Cooksey, Luann Alexander, Renee Jackson, Linda Winslett, and La Juana White, thank you so much for your patience.

To Shirley Patterson, Arleta "Pat" Houston, Kim Stewart, Carol Blackwell, and Julie Colbert, thanks for everything.

SAINTS, AIN'TS, AND SISTAHS

A Novel By

Toni J. Walker

SAINTS, AIN'TS, AND SISTAHS is a humorous, thrilling, and dramatic satire of four women who became acquainted at a Christian women's conference. The story depicts poignant and painful memories, tribulations, and victories of these women.

The primary character is Neisha, a reformed ex-convict and drug addict, who travels the highways and byways of Los Angeles to minister to the lost. Her husband, Barry, loves her "dirty drawers."

Bettye, an internationally acclaimed gospel singer, is the first lady of Agape Pentecostal Holiness Church in Atlanta, Georgia. Her musical talent is comparable to icons Aretha Franklin and Mahalia Jackson. Her three children, the result of her "street life," are momma's babies and daddy's maybes. Their biological fathers could be pimps, pastors, or politicians.

Marie's middle-class father, Aaron, raised her. Upon his demise, she inherited his estate. Marie weaved in and out of salvation like a basket maker, professing the gospel while clamoring for the glamour of the fast life. She has more skeletons in her closet than a cemetery.

Dae's (pronounced "day") name is contrary to her attitude and personality. She represents more darkness than light and more attitude than gratitude. Dae loves the party life, bad boys, drama, and the "Lawd" in that order. She misdirects an astronomical amount of her negative attitude and feelings toward Neisha. She appears intent on destroying everything positive in her life.

PROLOGUE

In Los Angeles, California, autumn of October 1995, Santa Ana Winds prevailed. The dry heat was humid and annoying. The wind mustered dirt and debris in its path as it breezed swiftly. Charcoaled ashes from nearby fires mingled with the wind, leaving a distinct smell of smoke in the air.

Near the Southern California Convention Center (SCCC), men and women waved red, green, and orange flags as they solicited customers to park in their respective parking lots. Their prices ranged from a maximum price of $10 to $15, a comparable bargain to the minimum $50 parking at the SCCC.

The sold-out venue at the SCCC was a Christian Women's Conference hosted by Prophetess Madeline Madison and several acclaimed speakers, singers, and evangelists. Outside, ticket scalpers hustled to sell outrageously priced tickets to desperate women who yearned to hear a spoken word or a song that might change their lives.

Inside the magnanimous building, women scurried about to locate various workshops. In the seminar, "Pregnant with Purpose," only four of the twenty women who enrolled were in attendance. They were Dae Denise Gordon, Bettye Michelle Stewart-Butler, Neisha Lynette Fuller, and Marie Danielle Johnson. The women attributed the mishap as God's intervention to bring them together. After all, God was not the orchestrator or coincidence.

The presenter was licensed evangelist Jenna Brown, Ph.D. She theologically reaffirmed that the women were born with a unique purpose for their lives. She also compared their pending trials and tribulations to the conception and birth of a child, the joy of conceiving, and the labor pains of birthing. Furthermore, she concluded that once they birthed their purpose that they would receive peace, at least for a while. Yet, she stipulated that as God's chosen, they would suffer from ongoing challenges of persecution and spiritual warfare more than others would.

The prophetically anointed Dr. Brown didn't disclose her discernment, which revealed that one of the four women would ultimately serve as a sacrifice for the others to fulfill their purpose.

The four women, Bettye, Dae, Marie, and Neisha immediately developed a spiritual bond of kinship that overrode the quaintness of their friendship. Each woman struggled immensely in her relationship with God.

Dae and Bettye were raised in church. At some point, they separated themselves from the church. Marie and Neisha were exposed to the secular ways of the world.

Initially, they referred to each other as sisters. However, feeling that the term was too vague, they selected the endearing term "sistahs." Jokingly, they made a "Sistahs Pact," an agreement among them to support each other unconditionally. The so-called joke became a serious journey in their lives.

The Sistahs' Pact

We, Dae Denise Gordon, Neisha Lynette Fuller, Bettye Michelle Stewart-Butler, and Marie Danielle Johnson signed this pact in unity as Sistahs in Christ.

Signatures:

Dae Denise Gordon

Bettye Michelle Stewart-Butler

Neisha Lynette Fuller

Marie Danielle Johnson

Signed and dated October 9, 1995, in Los Angeles, California.

Through the years, the sistahs developed and cultivated their friendship. However, the most significant relationship was that of Ms. Jenna and Neisha.

Jenna Brown was an extremely wealthy woman. She lived in an exquisite home, drove a luxury car, and wore modest but expensive clothing. She stopped using her married name, Porter, several years after her husband died. Since Brown was a common surname, people did not link her to the legacy of the illustrious Browns and Porters.

Very few of Jenna's associates and friends were aware of her family's ancestry. Among her ancestors were the first freed slaves who obtained property in the South after the Civil War and the so-called emancipation of slaves by President Abraham Lincoln.

Jenna's father, Franklin, was a scientist. He invented skin and hair products for Negroes. He also developed irrigation and agricultural instruments that helped Negro farmers nurture their crops and reap rewarding benefits.

Naomi, Jenna's mother, was one of the few so-called colored women in the South. She taught students in a log cabin that served as a schoolhouse. She was adamant that Jenna would obtain a college education and become a schoolteacher.

Isaiah Porter's family became the wealthiest Negro family in the United States during the post-Civil War Era. He was born with a tarnished silver spoon in his mouth. As an adult, Isaiah was a ruthless and conniving businessperson who was determined to financially increase his empire by whatever means necessary.

Isaiah, and Jenna's father Franklin, explored collaboration on several business ventures. Isaiah schemed to purchase several patents and inventions from Franklin that would substantially increase the Porter fortune.

Isaiah and Franklin came to an impasse. Franklin dedicated much of his energy and resources to empower the Negro race. Isaiah cared less about providing for people. He preferred to focus more on adding dollar signs and zeros to his bank account.

Franklin hesitated to conduct business with someone so ambitious, especially since Negroes needed support from their people. It was bad enough that they were discriminated against by others.

Isaiah decided that he might have an advantage with Franklin if his son, Andrew, hooked up with Jenna, Isaiah's daughter. He arranged to invite Frankin, Naomi, and Jenna to dinner.

Isaiah's plot to use Andrew in a scheme to date Jenna backfired. Andrew and Jenna fell madly in love. They got married after she graduated from college. The newlyweds moved into the Porter family ranch, a former slave plantation that sprawled on several acres of land in Jackson, Mississippi. Jenna taught school. Andrew worked as an executive for his father's company.

Isaiah immediately pressured Andrew and Jenna to start a family. He wanted an heir to his legacy, someone whom he would groom and control.

Andrew and Jenna did not need Isaiah's constant prodding. They tried desperately to have a baby because of their mutual love and desire to have children. Several months into their marriage, medical tests revealed that Andrew was sterile.

Isaiah threw a tantrum. To say that he was upset was an understatement. He verbally emasculated Andrew and challenged his son's masculinity. He disregarded Andrew's feelings. His worry was predicated on obtaining a male heir to his legacy.

Overwhelmed with feelings of shame and embarrassment, Andrew enrolled in the army to prove his manhood to his father and distance himself from Isaiah's wrath.

Jenna begged Andrew to reconsider his decision. She tried to convince him that they did not need his father's approval or wealth. Andrew abandoned Jenna and joined the army.

Jenna remained with Andrew's family. She continued to teach.

Isaiah demanded that Jenna learn the family business. She had quite an acumen for business. He attempted to persuade her to join the business as vice president, to no avail.

A year after his enlistment, Andrew's parents died in a car accident. He inherited everything. As the sole male heir to the Porter legacy, the government gave him the option of receiving an honorable discharge and returning home. He chose to remain in the service. He was not ready to resume his role as husband. Andrew, much like his father, allowed his self-centered ego to drive his emotions.

Andrew received a promotion to sergeant. He was the only Black officer amongst a group of racist White soldiers. Most of them hated him because he was handsome and wealthy. The promotion fueled their hatred even more. A few months later, White members of Andrew's troop shot him. They reported to their commanding officers that Andrew was killed by "friendly fire", that it was an accident.

Jenna was devastated. Of course, the fact that she inherited substantial wealth did not console her. She sold the Porter Estate but maintained a controlling interest in the company. She invested substantial amounts of money in many of her father's business ventures. Several produced a large financial payoff. Financially, she was set for life.

Jenna moved from Mississippi to Los Angeles. She became a member of Arlington Holiness Community Church. She taught grammar school students at the church academy. Her existence centered on work, church, and ministry.

Jenna lived a reclusive lifestyle. She rarely traveled. She attended very few social functions. The loss of family and loved ones left her feeling abandoned and alone. She did not allow anyone to cross her emotional boundaries.

Yet from the moment that Jenna met Neisha, she felt attracted to Neisha's free spirit. As time passed, they bonded and developed a type of mother-daughter relationship. Neisha affectionately called her Ms. Jenna.

Nine Years Later

Jackson's Funeral Home is a two-story, green and white, Spanish-style stucco building located in Inglewood, California. The building encompasses an entire block. A large sign displays the name of the funeral home in large, bold, and colorful letters visible to traffic traveling on La Brea Avenue. Stained glass windows of luminous colors project a church-like edifice from the second floor of the building. Yellow and red rose bushes beautify the patio seating area. Several hearses are parked in the adjacent lot.

Jackson's Funeral Home holds a legacy as the first Negro owned and operated funeral home in the northwestern United States. It was established circa the early 1930s. The initial ideology of the owners was that folks of color, even those born in poverty, desired to leave this earth in grandeur style and fashion. During that era, people purchased life insurance shortly after the birth of their children. The sum of money spent on funerals often outweighed any other large financial expense during their lives.

For more than half a century, Jackson's Funeral Home prepared celebrities, politicians, and the community at large for their homegoing services. The ownership of the funeral home has been maintained by generations of family members.

In early September 2004, the temperature was a raging 102 degrees. The humid and hot weather provided little, if any, solace in the shade. Only in Los Angeles could such an atmosphere exist when autumn was a few weeks away.

As Neisha Fuller-Garrett slowly climbed up the stairs of Jackson's Funeral Home, she felt overwhelmed by the weather.

Neisha recalled several of her mother's clichés on miserably hot days. Her mother might have stated, "Neisha, it is so hot outside that you could fry an egg on the sidewalk." On the other hand, she might have said, "Even the devil's wife can't stand the heat. If you stick a needle in the ground, you can hear her screaming."

As a child, Neisha took her mother's sayings as gospel. On a few occasions, she attempted to fry eggs on the sidewalk. The results were a nasty, gooey mess. Neisha also experimented with sticking a needle in the ground and poised her ear to hear the devil's wife scream. She burned her ear. Neisha concluded that her mother's sayings were old wives' tales.

At the top of the stairs, Neisha paused long enough to retrieve a tissue from her purse. She gently wiped away the miniscule beads of perspiration that glistened on her forehead and neck.

Inside the building, Neisha stood under a vent and sought refuge from the heat and humidity. She slightly opened the neckline of her blouse and allowed the cool air to caress her hot, sticky, and clammy skin.

Images flooded Neisha's mind of cool air flowing from the vents to keep the corpses from turning into melted zombies, something reminiscent of a Halloween horror movie or sci-fi thriller.

The distorted images prompted Neisha to laugh. The luxury of laughter had been missing in her life with the traumatic experiences that she recently endured. She embraced the levity for a few brief moments, knowing that it would be replaced by grief once she entered the funeral home.

Neisha approached a beautiful mahogany complexion woman who sat behind a glass and chrome oval-shaped desk in the lobby of the funeral home.

A badge on the lapel of the woman's navy blue silk jacket identified her as Myisha Coleman. Her eyes were fixated on the latest issue of "Ebony Magazine". Slightly startled by Neisha's sudden presence, Myisha looked up and smiled. She revealed teeth so white and perfect that she should have starred in a toothpaste commercial.

Myisha asked, "May I help you?"

Neisha replied, "Yes. Please tell me where the viewing room is for Marie Danielle Johnson."

Myisha pointed and answered. "Ma'am, Ms. Johnson is in *Viewing Room 2*. Turn to your right and follow the yellow arrows on the floor. The room is at the end of the hallway."

Intimidated by her less-than-perfect teeth, Neisha smiled slightly and replied, "Thanks".

Neisha pivoted and strolled down the hallway until she located *Viewing Room 2*. She entered.

Bettye and Dae sat a few feet away from the casket. Neisha approached the casket and stared at Marie's lifeless body for several moments. She shook her head in dismay.

Holding back tears, Neisha greeted Betty and Dae with hugs. She sat next to Bettye.

Bettye appeared to be ensconced in a trance.

Dae appeared to be under the influence.

Silence permeated the room. It was so quiet that you could have heard a rat piss on cotton.

15

During stressful times, Neisha often has bouts of anxiety and chatters excessively. After a few moments had passed, she could no longer endure the silence and tension in the room. Her anxiety surfaced.

With her eyes fixated on Marie's casket, Neisha asked Bettye and Dae, "What would happen if you were not living saved and holy at the time of your death? If you were fornicating, lusting, or busting moves in the club when your soul left your body, where would you spend eternal life?"

Bettye tried to speak, but grief held her tongue hostage. She could not believe that Marie lay dead in the casket in front of her, or the horrendous circumstances surrounding Marie's death.

Dae did not care to think about eternal life. She had enough challenges with her earthly existence. She frequently and unsuccessfully tried to balance sin and salvation on equal scales.

Neisha retreated to her thoughts. Being ever mindful of God's grace and mercy, she reflected on her salvation. Cognizant that the motionless body in the casket could have been hers, Neisha silently thanked God for sparing her life one more time. She prayed that Marie repented before she died.

Neisha recalled a conversation that she had with Marie several weeks before Marie's death.

Marie stated, "Neisha, sometimes life is not all that it is cracked up to be. If I die first, put me in the casket face down and on my stomach. I want to show some folks where they can kiss for the last time."

"Marie, do you realize that you cannot enter the Kingdom of Heaven like that?"

"Ne, I am a backslider. Unless major changes occur in my life, the last place that I will spend eternity is heaven. I will not be walking the streets of gold. Instead, I'll be hovering over hot coals."

Neisha began to cry. She asked, "Do you want to talk about it?

A tear escaped from Marie's right eye.

"No, Neisha. Just keep praying for a sistah."

The exterior of the pine casket boasted a glossy pink shellacked finish. Attached on each side were three sturdy, solid brass handles for pallbearers to transport Marie to the hearse and gravesite.

Bouquets and wreaths of carnations and roses surrounded the casket. The room was filled with a fragrant, flowery aroma. Marie lay inside the casket with her head propped on a pink satin pillow. Several strands of imitation white pearls accessorized her red, scooped-neck dress. Only two to three eyelashes appeared on each tightly shut eyelid. Her eyebrows were drawn in an imperfect arch. The oval shape present in both cheeks indicated that she might have tried to scream before her death. Yet, her thin lips perched a menacing and frightening grin.

Neisha walked towards the casket. She removed a laminated, miniature copy of "The Sistahs' Pact" from her purse. She placed it on the left side of Marie's body near her heart.

Neisha murmured, "Rest in peace, my sistah."

Tears streamed down Neisha's face. She planted a kiss on Marie's cold forehead. The makeup foundation left an unpleasant, chalky taste on her lips. She swiped her lips with her tongue and returned to her seat.

Dae sat on the opposite side of Bettye. Before she embarked on her journey to the funeral home, she swallowed a couple of bluish green antidepressant pills with two short dog liquor bottles of cognac. She felt blitzed. Neisha's sanctimonious philosophy was blowing her high.

Dae sighed. She staggered slightly as she walked towards the casket. She popped a fart and giggled. Without a tinge of embarrassment, she slurred, "Well, better out than in."

Bettye and Neisha gave her disapproving looks.

Dae stood over the casket and visually inventoried Marie's appearance.

Dissatisfied, she stated, "Dam, I need to fix Marie's hair."

Dae's long, thin, manicured fingers rummaged through her brown leather designer purse until she located a black rubber comb. As Dae styled Marie's hair, she sighed and rolled her eyes at Neisha.

"You know that I can't stand cheap, synthetic hair. God knows that you could have afforded to buy human hair."

Neisha retorted, "I do not recall you spending one cent towards the cost of Marie's funeral. It is not too late for you to purchase a new wig that is more suitable for your taste."

Bettye maintained her silence.

Frustrated, Dae continued combing the reddish-brown wig. Suddenly, the comb tangled in several strands of hair. As Dae tried to disentangle it, the wig flew off Marie's head and landed on the floor. The scarred tissue on Marie's face revealed where Ron bludgeoned her with a bat during his reign of terror.

Dae sobered up enough to scream, "Oh my God!"

Dae felt an urge to run and pick up the wig, but her footsteps were frozen.

Bettye and Neisha ran to the side of the casket and stood near Dae. The women stared at Marie's disfigured face and sobbed hysterically.

Finally, Bettye broke her silence.

"It was bad enough that Ron shot Marie several times. I cannot believe that sadistic bastard also bludgeoned her with a bat. He was not simply crazy, his ass was insane."

Neisha nodded her head in agreement. She chimed in. "Ron lost control of his senses. The police called Marie's death a brutal crime of rage and passion. They could not give an exact number of how many times he hit Marie. He shot her four times. He left two bullets in the chamber. He successfully blew his brains out with one of the bullets."

Neisha withheld some of the gruesome details concerning Marie's death. Ron hit Marie with so much force that her skull cracked. Pieces of her brain were found next to her body.

For a change, Dae kept her damn mouth shut.

As Bettye and Neisha returned to their seats, they exchanged comments about how Marie no longer suffered. They agreed that Ron's soul should burn in hell.

Somewhat composed, Dae retrieved the wig from the floor. She was determined to make Marie look presentable.

Neisha observed Dae labor for several minutes.

"Dae, give it a break. You are going to comb the hair from the seams of that wig. I cannot believe these idiots did not glue the wig on Marie's head. They have enough experience dealing with Black folks to know how dramatic we can get at funerals. Shoot, folks fall over the casket and grab at the body. I went to a funeral where some fool woman tried to get into the casket with the corpse. She screamed, 'Lord, not my baby. Take me instead.' That crazy heifer knew that she didn't want to swap places with a dead person."

Neisha paused for several seconds.

"Don't y'all sit there acting all brand new. You've seen those funeral phonies. They did not show love when the person was alive. At the funeral, they are the main ones who act like fools. They whoop and holler like that trifling ass daughter in the movie, "Imitation of Life." Some act as if they are auditioning for a movie. They cry, sling snot, and lie. Miss me with that drama. Give me flowers while I am living, and don't perpetrate a lie when I die."

Bettye stated, "Neisha, you are so crazy."

Neisha replied, "Maybe, but I'm not stupid."

Tears of sorrow streamed down Neisha's face as she reminisced.

"I really miss my mother and Ms. Jenna."

Dae retorted, "I can understand the tears for your mother. But your life is much better now with all the money that you inherited from Jenna."

If Neisha's dark chocolate skin could have turned beet red from rage, it would have.

Neisha angrily stormed towards Dae.

Bettye grabbed Neisha's arm.

"Neisha, do not entertain the devil. Dae has been on a tangent ever since she arrived."

Dae became defensive. She rolled her eyes at Bettye and Neisha.

"Bettye, you always take Neisha's side. I was not talking to you. My name is Dae, not devil."

"Devil or Dae, whatever. Shut your mouth. I am not feeling your drama today. I cannot believe that you came to Marie's viewing under the influence. You give new meaning to miserable. You should have your own show called, 'Hot, Miserable Mess'."

Neisha spoke up.

"Dae, don't hate. You deliberately bring out the worst in people. You need to thank God that I am sober and saved. If not, I would go straight hood on you. If you want to play the dozens, maybe your mother should have named you "Night" for the darkness that you represent. You certainly do not represent light or day. When you leave here, go find a 12-step or prayer meeting."

Bettye released Neisha's arm.

Neisha walked behind Dae. She gently slapped the back of Dae's head.

"Dae remember that favor ain't always fair."

Bettye suppressed the urge to laugh.

Dae stood at the casket, speechless.

Bettye shook her head in disbelief. She could not fathom how Neisha tolerated Dae regularly.

When they first met, each of the four women proclaimed a desire to do God's will per His plan for her life. They were involved in ministry and outreach. Yet, even from the start, it appeared that Dae and Marie had hidden agendas.

Over the years, the fire for ministry in Dae's life began to extinguish. She often put God's will in low priority to her whims and desires. It would take a helluva match to rekindle her flame.

Marie struggled with balancing her secular needs and wants with her spiritual purpose. She talked a good game. However, walking the walk was different. She served more lip action than hip action. Unfortunately, poor Marie had run out of chances.

Bettye's eyes roamed from the casket to the viewing room door. She anticipated her mother's unwelcome appearance to swindle her for money. The fact that Bettye was in town to pay her final respects to her departed friend would not deter her scandalous mother.

Bettye grabbed her purse.

"Ladies, I need fresh air. I am going outside for a while."

As she exited the building, Betty's eyes filled with tears. She was not emotionally equipped for the magnitude of sorrow and despair that she encountered in *Viewing Rom 2*.

Outside near the rosebushes, Bettye located a secluded area of the parking lot. She dialed *54 on her cellular phone and plugged in her secret code. A recorded message stated, "Your mailbox is full."

All the messages were from her mother, Janice. In the last message, Janice screamed with indignant venom in her voice.

"Bettye, I need money. I suggest that you deposit money in my account immediately. I know that you are in Los Angeles for Marie's funeral, although I cannot imagine why. She tried to act all holy and righteous, but she was just an adulterous tramp banging another woman's husband. My heart bleeds for Ron's wife. It is a shame that good women such as she and I suffer because hot tail heifers will not stay away from other women's husbands."

Bettye yelled back into the phone, although no one was on the other end.

"Janice, one of my best friends is dead. How could you say those horrible things? If your heart bleeds anything, it must be oil or water."

Furious, Bettye erased the messages. Janice had no right to condemn anyone. Perhaps, if she and some of those other self-righteous biddies spent less time in numerous church auxiliaries and other folks' business, their husbands might stay faithful.

Betty telephoned her husband, David. He did not answer. Perplexed and disappointed, she left a voice message and placed the phone in her purse.

Bettye returned inside the funeral home.

Introducing the Sistahs

Bettye was born and raised in the 9th ward of Houston, Texas. Her mother, Janice, made a decent and honest income as a beautician. Janice held down the financial responsibilities of the household. Janice was one of those church busybodies who could always speak on what was wrong with other people's relationships, but her marriage was a joke.

Bettye's father, Chester, spent money as fast as Janice earned it. On any given day, he might be at a local juke joint gambling, shooting dice, or playing pool. The money that he did not waste on gambling, he spent on whiskey and women.

The family resided in a home owned by Nanna, Bettye's maternal grandmother. Nanna did everything in her power to create a loving environment. Any nurturing that Bettye received came from Nanna.

Bettye was eight years old when Chester died. A car hit him as he drunkenly stumbled across the street after leaving an afterhours night spot at 5 a.m. His mistress, Chantal, accompanied him. She escaped unharmed.

When Chantal and her two illegitimate children by Chester arrived at the funeral, she insisted that they sit in the section cordoned off for family.

Before Chester's death, Janice was clueless about his extended family. When she got a glimpse of Little Chester, Janice became enraged. Little Chester was the spitting image of his father. To add insult to injury, Janice got a glimpse of Chester's side piece. She could not believe that Chester cheated on her with a Jezebel.

Chantal was the opposite of Janice. Chantal wore a long blonde wig, a short mini dress, and fishnet-style stockings. She looked like she had just left a nightclub.

A huge scene ensued.

Janice looked Chantal up and down. She yelled, "Get your homewrecking ass out of here."

Chantal yelled back. "I ain't going nowhere. Chester was the father of my children, and he was my man."

People looked at them, waiting for the next round - some laughed, some whispered.

Janice did not say another word. She was embarrassed enough.

The ushers politely asked Chantal to move. She sat a few rows behind Janice and the other family members.

After Chester's death, Janice and Bettye attended church on Sunday and twice during the week. Bettye's young mind could not comprehend why, especially since Janice was angry with God for taking her husband. She also failed to understand how her mother, a Christian woman, could be so miserable.

To keep her mind off her problems, Bettye joined the youth choir. Her talent far exceeded her years on earth. She put her heart, soul, and pain into her music. She sang like an angel.

Janice showed pride and admiration when people complimented Bettye's gifts. She had the audacity to walk around with her chest all puffed up like a proud, loving mother.

Away from church, Janice consistently berated Bettye. She called her lazy, ugly, and no good. She told Bettye that she would never amount to anything, just like her father.

Bettye was Janice's only biological child, but Janice treated her like a stepchild. Bettye had to cook a full dinner every evening after school, sweep and mop the floors, and wash and dry the dishes. She did the household laundry every week. In addition, she was expected to help at the beauty shop, do her homework, and get As and Bs at school.

Living under the same roof as Janice became intolerable. Bettye ran away and found refuge with her paternal uncles and their women. They were involved in street life and various sorts of illicit and illegal activities. They were gamblers, pimps, and hustlers.

Despite her Christian upbringing, Bettye soon became involved with drugs and prostitution. Her drug of choice was heroin. Her sexual orientation was bisexual.

During that dysfunctional course of life, Bettye bore three children. Teresa, Bettye's firstborn, was born addicted to heroin. Children's Protective Services immediately detained the baby at the hospital. Bettye's other two children were drug exposed as well. They were detained at birth.

Her Nanna insisted that her great grandchildren would not go to a foster home. She forced Janice to bring each child home from the hospital. Janice begrudgingly assumed the role of

29

caregiver for the children. She knew better than to cross Nanna.

Periodically, Bettye cleaned herself up and visited her children and grandmother. Each time she left her children, it broke her heart. They stood near the door, cried, and begged her not to go.

After several years, Bettye gave up the street life. Her pimp, Pretty T, murdered one of his hookers because she chose a new pimp. Bettye feared that she would die or face some other wretched demise if she continued that lifestyle.

Like a prodigal child, Bettye moved back home with her mother, grandmother, and three children. Nanna prayed for her and nursed her through the drug withdrawals. Bettye kicked her heroin habit, cold turkey. After she became sober, she planned to reclaim custody of her children, obtain welfare assistance, and apply for low-income housing.

Janice vetoed Bettye's decision. She taunted Bettye.

"Girl, you must have trifling genetics just like your father. Nobody in my family has ever been on welfare. It will not start with you taking handouts. Before that happens, I will apply for full custody of those kids through the court. Any right-minded judge will give those children to a hard working Christian widow rather than a dopehead whore of a mother."

Outraged by Janice's holier-than-thou attitude, Bettye became further determined to raise her children. Bettye realized that finding employment would be difficult, but not impossible. She had intellect and street education. She obtained a fake copy of a high school diploma and applied for jobs at several temporary agencies. Eventually, she became employed as a file clerk for a law firm.

Things were going well. Bettye focused on being a good mother. She contributed financially to the household, which decreased Janice's cynicism. She passed the equivalency test for her high school diploma and enrolled in community college. She majored in music.

The last thing on Bettye's mind was an intimate relationship. She witnessed enough drama, abuse, and toxic relationships to last a lifetime. She enjoyed her status as a happy, single mother with children.

Mutual friends introduced Bettye to David Butler, a successful, handsome, single White psychologist and preacher. He pastored a huge congregation in Atlanta, Georgia. He was a workaholic, married to his work.

After several dates, David became enamored with Bettye. He commuted from Georgia to Texas regularly to be with her. Nine months later, they eloped. She and her children relocated to Atlanta.

Janice pretended to be happy that Bettye and the children were no longer a part of her life. In reality, she resented her daughter and despised the fact that Bettye was happily married, especially to a White man. Janice also missed her grandchildren.

The first few years of David and Bettye's marriage were extremely difficult. David lost members of his congregation and clients from his practice. The family received death threats. The Klan burned a cross in their front yard. Bettye's children could not attend the local, segregated White school and traveled a great distance to attend an all Black school. Yet, their love for God and each other helped them persevere through it all.

After things had settled down, Bettye returned to school and obtained a bachelor's degree in music. She resumed singing and began writing songs. She auditioned for acclaimed writer, producer, and playwright Chris Taylor. Her performance was outstanding. Bettye became a headliner in his venues. Her music and acting careers skyrocketed. She recorded several top-selling gospel music albums.

Bettye's children have thrived. One of the best choices that she made was to take custody of her children from Janice.

Dae

The Bible warns against prideful and boastful spirits. Dae possessed both. She held her education and attractive looks in such high esteem that she often acted snobby towards others. Yet, despite her formal education, Dae often lacked the use of common sense and humility. She was bougie.

At one point, Dae's granny tried to set her straight.

"Young lady, you are too damn smart for your own good. You think that book smarts override good, old-fashioned common sense. Trust me that there ain't no fool like an educated one."

Dae flippantly answered back.

"Granny, I am smart enough to know that there is nothing common or old-fashioned about me."

Dae grew up in a Victorian-Tudor style home with her siblings and parents, Leroy and Gladys.

Leroy worked as an electrician for the city. He was domineering. Whatever he said in the home was law. He was a chain cigarette smoker and drank occasionally.

Gladys worked for the postal service. Saved and sanctified, she did not drink or smoke. She said her body was a holy temple and nothing would defile it. She was the consummate passive, submissive wife.

Together, Leroy and Gladys ran an authoritative household. The children were forbidden to play outside or watch television during the week.

In high school, Dae occasionally sneaked out of the house and went to a party or dance. More often than not, her parents or siblings woke up during the night and realized she was gone. The consequences of her actions usually resulted in punishment from two weeks to one month. Dae gladly accepted the punishment in exchange for a good time.

While in college, despite all her partying, fraternizing, and socializing, Dae graduated with honors. She received several lucrative job offers before graduating.

Dae and Mark Roberts met at a Christmas party. He worked as an aeronautical engineer for a major aircraft company. In addition to being intelligent and handsome, Mark earned good money. He served on the board of directors at his church and was one of the pastor's distinguished consultants.

Dae fell head over heels in love. She and Mark became inseparable. She retired from her position as a social butterfly. She committed her life to Christ and joined Mark's church. Although they maintained separate residences for appearance's sake, after all, he was a man of God But behind closed doors, they indulged in fornication.

On their wedding day, the beautifully decorated church was crowded with Mark and Dae's family and friends. Mark's best man, dressed in a designer tuxedo, stood at the altar. He held the wedding ring in his right hand and patiently waited for Mark to join him.

Dae resembled a professional model on the cover of a wedding magazine. She stood at the head of the aisle, waiting to make the grand entrance that

34

she had rehearsed several times. Leroy stood by her side. They waited for Mark.

After a sufficient amount of time had passed, it became evident that Mark had abandoned Dae. Leroy, Gladys, and Dae retreated to the pastor's office and discussed options. Leroy re-entered the sanctuary and dismissed the guests.

Dae, Gladys, and Granny went home. Leroy, filled with rage, roamed the city looking for Mark. As the bride's parents, he and Gladys spent good, hard-earned money on a wedding.

Leroy kept his shotgun in the trunk of his car. Fortunately for Mark, Leroy did not find him.

After her unimaginable wedding fiasco, Dae sought revenge against men. Her mission in life became to love them and leave them. She was determined to give them a taste of the hurtful medicine that Mark gave her.

Dae was also angry with God for allowing her to be humiliated and heartbroken. She stopped attending the same church where she and Mark were previously members. Primarily, she became an E.T.C. (Easter, Thanksgiving, and Christmas) churchgoer. Occasionally, she volunteered with a few ministries and auxiliaries.

Dae no longer maintained a personal relationship with God. She rarely prayed and never fasted. She reclaimed her crown as a social butterfly. and fed her fleshly desires as opposed to her spirit.

Dae relocated to Los Angeles.

Neisha

Neisha was born and raised in Los Angeles, California in a diverse neighborhood of homeowners, renters, retired seniors, single parents, middle class working people, and welfare recipients.

Shortly after Neisha was born, her mother, Dottie, busted her father, Charles, with another woman. Rather than show remorse, Charles assaulted Dottie for "spying on him". He told her to get out of his home and take her child with her.

Fearful for her and Neisha's lives, Dottie went to a phone booth and called the police. When officers arrived, they escorted Dottie and Neisha home. Since the lease and bills were in Charles' name, officers could not force him to leave unless Dottie wanted to press charges against him for assault. She did not.

Officers waited while Dottie packed a few bags. The police transported Dottie and her toddler daughter to the apartment of Neisha's godmother. The woman excitedly welcomed them as she despised Charles.

Dottie filed for divorce. She did not ask for alimony or child support.

Five years later, Charles reappeared in Neisha's life. He became significantly involved in the role of father, providing financial and emotional contributions.

Neisha was seven years old when Charles married Karla, the mother of his two younger daughters. Charles' involvement in Neisha's life decreased. Her true colors shined. Karla pretended to want the best for Neisha until she married Charles. Afterwards, she complained that Charles spent too much time and money on Neisha. Several times, when she was alone with Neisha, Karla would pinch or hit Neisha for no apparent reason. Of course, Neisha did not tell Dottie because she knew all hell would break loose, and he would not be able to visit Charles.

A year or so later, Neisha telephoned Charles to schedule their weekly visit. The phone was disconnected. She persuaded Dottie to take her to his house. It was vacant. Charles and his family had disappeared. The link to the paternal side of her legacy was suddenly gone. Neisha was devastated.

The maternal side of Neisha's family gave a new meaning to dysfunctional kinfolk. As Neisha grew older and became more aware of the family's history, she was convinced that a generational curse existed.

In the early 1950s, Neisha's family transported her great, great Uncle Jimmy out of San Antonio, Texas, in a casket to save his life. Ku Klux Klan members sought to kill him after he beat up a redneck cracker for spitting in his face and calling him "boy." Midway out of the city, when he was out of danger, the family put him on a bus to California. Jimmy, always paranoid that White folks were out to get him, died at the age of 39 from cirrhosis of the liver. He drank himself to death.

Louise, Neisha's maternal grandmother, claimed to be a devout Baptist. She attended church every Sunday and sang in several choirs. Since Neisha and Dottie were not committed to attending church, Louise repeatedly told them that they were heathens. She claimed that her only daughter and granddaughter were destined to die and go to hell.

Neisha's grandfather, Samuel, identified himself as an outstanding member of the community, a lodge member, and a deacon of the church. Behind his back, people called him "Cheatin' Deacon Stanford."

Apparently, going to church on Sundays did not exorcise Louise of her demons. Louise certainly believed in distilled spirits, scotch whiskey being her favorite.

To this day, Neisha occasionally laughs when she recalls memories of her grandmother.

"Neisha, look in my purse and get my pressure medication. Don't forget to grab me a glass and some milk for my scotch. I need something to kill the nasty taste of these pills."

Louise was engaged in an adulterous affair with an elder of the same church. One Sunday after service, the elder's jealous wife approached Louise from behind and stabbed her to death with an ice pick. Unfortunately, Louise missed the opportunity to retrieve her .38 caliber gun from her purse. Everyone knew that Louise packed her pistol everywhere that she went, including church. Obviously, it only made sense that someone would get the drop on her and leave her defenseless.

After Louise's death, Deacon Stanford became ashamed to show his face in public despite his long history of cheating on his wife. He suffered a massive heart attack and died three months after Louise was murdered.

Neisha's childhood was daunting. Her mother, Dottie, did not display a lot of affection toward her only daughter. Her parenting skills were minimal. Obviously, Edward and Louise were not the best of role models.

Yet, despite the lack of kisses and hugs that Neisha did not receive from Dottie, her mother would tear that butt up when Neisha misbehaved. As if the whippings were not physically painful enough, Neisha received an emotional spanking as well.

Dottie forced Neisha to get switches from one specific tree that belonged to Mrs. Denker.

Mrs. Denker attended church every Sunday. Yet, she raised hell all during the week. She was a crotchety old woman in her sixties who did not want anyone coming near her home, much less climbing her tree. She usually caught Neisha perched on the tree, grabbing a switch.

On one occasion, Mrs. Denker stood on her front porch with her hands firmly planted on her huge hips and yelled a string of obscenities and insults.

"Hey, gal, I told you to keep your black, nappy-headed ass off my tree. I hope you break your damn neck. Get down and go tell yo mammy not to send you down here no more."

Neisha politely replied, "Yes, ma'am."

Neisha grabbed the switch and ran home to tell Dottie.

Dottie put her hair in a ponytail and slipped on her fluffy, raggedy, furry blue house shoes. By the time she arrived at Mrs. Denker's house four doors away, Mrs. Denker had locked all the doors and windows and refused to make her presence known.

The irony is that although Mrs. Denker cursed out Neisha and talked about her mama, she repeatedly invited Neisha to church.

Dottie told Neisha, "You are not going anywhere with that wanna be saint. She is just another ain't who may or may not get into heaven."

When Mrs. Denker became senile, Dottie never observed anyone visit the home, including church folks. Cantankerous Mrs. Denker was all alone. Dottie made sure that Neisha took her food. Neisha left the food on the porch and rang the doorbell. They kept watch on her.

Overall, young Neisha's exposure to church folks was tainted. She developed a sour attitude towards the people who represented the church and religion. She understood why Dottie did not feel a need to attend church every Sunday to know God.

Aside from the drama with Mrs. Denker and her mother, Neisha endured unbearable taunting from her peers at school. They often ridiculed her because Dottie could not afford to buy her expensive clothing and toys.

Being the darkest-skinned girl on the block made matters even more complicated. Neisha's first introduction to hate and prejudice came from her own race. Many of the light-skinned children could not play with her because of her dark skin and socioeconomic status. Some people considered her skin pigment an abomination or a curse. Others used it as a weapon to make her feel inferior.

Hence, Neisha was desperate to change her skin tone and features. She tried extreme measures such as adding bleach and homogenized milk to her bath. Neisha also used her allowance to purchase skin-bleaching cream. She broke out in hives. Her face resembled a large chocolate-covered strawberry with prickles. She refused to leave the house. Finally, Neisha resigned herself to the fact that she would be dark-skinned for the remainder of her earthly life.

Yet, Neisha had not completely given up on making some form of external change to her body. She tried to reshape her nose by sleeping with a clothespin on it. The result was physical pain added to her mental anguish.

During early adulthood, Neisha's body blossomed. She referred to this as her "got it" phase. She got booty, legs, and a lot of male attention. She got buck wild. Her "got it" phase contributed to self-destruction, drugs, and prison. After her discharge from prison, she shook most of her bad habits, like partying and doing drugs.

Fornication remained one of her strongholds. Sexual activity often left her feeling guilty and sinful. She enjoyed the instant gratification but hated the spiritual anguish. She prayed that the Rapture did not occur while she lay butt-naked and unmarried with some man.

Neisha is currently happily married to the love of her life, Barry, or so it seems.

Marie

Before her untimely demise, a fitting description of Marie may have been a beautiful "red-boned" Mulatto woman with green eyes. Her shoulder length, reddish brown hair was straight like white folks. She had classic, flawless beauty compared to Dorothy Dandridge or Lena Horne. Her brick house body complemented her appearance. When she entered a room, men and women paused to stare. Yet, Marie considered her beauty more of a curse than a blessing.

Marie's mother died during childbirth. Her father, Aaron, nearly died of grief. Initially, he wrestled with the thought of giving Marie up for adoption. Instead, he decided to take on the challenge of single fatherhood.

Aaron worked as a supervisor for a large automobile manufacturing plant in Detroit, Michigan. He earned good money. Marie never wanted for anything that Aaron could provide.

Marie learned how to manipulate the opposite sex at an early age. Often, she sat in her father's lap and reached deep into his pockets. She touched the hard thing that extended in the crouch of his pants. Whenever she asked him what it was, he laughed. As it became harder, she laughed. She thought it was a game. Aaron began rewarding her with gifts for playing their special game. Over time, Aaron inappropriately touched her "cookie. He told her to keep their game a secret.

As a teenager, Marie became aware that law and nature forbade her and Aaron's behavior. She confronted him.

"Daddy, our gym teachers gave a sex education lecture after two girls were busted in the shower touching each other inappropriately. Our teachers told us to report anyone who touches our private parts."

Aaron's neck muscles tightened. His veins bulged. Tension shot through his body.

"I never gave my permission for anyone to talk to you about sexual education."

"Daddy, that is not the issue. What we have been doing is wrong. It is not a game."

Aaron sobbed deeply. His entire body shook as he spoke.

"Baby, you are right. I am sorry. I miss your mother so much. You are the spitting image of her. Touching you makes me feel as though she is still here. I am a man. I have needs."

Feeling pity for Aaron, Marie kissed him on the mouth.

Aaron passionately returned the kiss. At that moment, he stole her virginity and innocence.

Aaron and Marie engaged in incestuous behavior. Marie became pregnant. She got an illegal abortion, which left her sterile.

Subsequently, Marie and Aaron quit having intimate relations. They feared that if the authorities found out, Aaron would go to prison and Marie would go to a foster home.

However, Marie's many years of sexual activity with her father went unfulfilled. Aaron was her first lover. Although what they did was wrong, she still desired the orgasms and feelings of intimacy. She was obsessed with sex. She needed, wanted, and had to have sex. Unfortunately, the young men at school became her prey.

Marie dated Jefferson McDaniel, the captain of Carver High School's Football Team. She stole Jefferson's virginity. She dated several other team members. Her promiscuity was revealed after several of the young men became infected with gonorrhea.

Marie had few female associates while growing up. Overall, her female cohorts could not stand her. Many were jealous of her good looks and shapely figure. Others did not want to be associated with the school whore.

Marie was nineteen years old when she married Matthew Solomon, a high-profile attorney. He specialized in entertainment law. Matthew was 20 years her senior and physically resembled Aaron. The men were approximately the same height and weight.

Matthew truly loved Marie. He tried his best to make their marriage work, although she committed adultery. It appeared to him that she might have been a nymphomaniac or sex addict. She could not get enough sex. She also wanted to experiment with kinky stuff such as whips and bondage. He did not want to inflict pain on her, or vice versa. His attempts to persuade her to seek therapy were futile.

After three challenging years, Matthew divorced Marie on the grounds of adultery and irreconcilable differences. He agreed to pay her alimony for three years if she did not remarry.

Marie moved in with Lester Griggs. They were involved in an adulterous affair during her marriage to Matthew. Lester owned a successful restaurant and catering business. His clientele was the elite of Detroit. Celebrities, athletes, and politicians frequented his establishment. He catered private parties in their homes.

Marie and Lester engaged in couple swapping and orgies. During one of those swaps, Lester became infatuated with Marie's friend, Elena. He broke up with Marie. Karma reared its ugly head.

A void remained in Marie's life that she felt only a man could fill. She decided a Christian man might be the answer. After church hopping for several months, she joined the Southern Community of Saints Holiness Church in Detroit. She joined for the wrong reasons. The items least on her agenda were repentance and deliverance, or to ask God for forgiveness for her past sins. She joined because of her attraction to the style of dress, the choir, and men.

Wendell Kelley, the lead choir director, became Marie's second husband. Wendell appeared to have slightly feminine ways. He was flamboyant in fashion and soft-spoken. The rumors were that Wendell was gay, or at the very least, bisexual. Marie chose not to believe the gossip and attributed it to jealousy. She attributed Wendell's characteristics to charisma, creativity, and talent.

Two years into their marriage, Marie decided to surprise Wendell with an afternoon rendezvous. When she arrived home, she heard two male voices in the kitchen. Not thinking much of it, she proceeded to enter. Shocked and dismayed, she found Wendell and his male lover, a drummer at the church, semi-dressed in a compromising position.

Marie ran upstairs and grabbed the .45 caliber revolver from the closet. Like a maniac, she proceeded down the stairs, shouting and shooting.

"Wendell, I am going to kill you and your queer ass boyfriend."

Her shots were in vain. The men had begun their escape. They drove off in Wendell's car.

Marie gathered logs and gasoline from the shed in the backyard and set a huge bonfire. She laughed hysterically at the crackling sounds of Wendell's clothes and personal belongings as the items were desecrated in a blaze of flaming glory.

The following day, Marie immediately went to her doctor and was tested for venereal diseases. Fortunately, the results were negative.

Marie never heard from Wendell again. Their attorneys finalized the divorce.

Marie nearly had a nervous breakdown. To say that she was devastated was an understatement. She was done with men. She realized that her relationships with the opposite sex were toxic. She had a sado-masochistic desire to hurt men and allow them to hurt her.

Feeling depressed and downtrodden, Marie returned home to live with Aaron. He died a year later. She received an annuity from his life insurance policy. She sold the house in Detroit. She felt that God had not forsaken her after all. Marie promised to be faithful to God and never commit adultery again.

Marie moved to the palm tree-lined streets of sunny Los Angeles. The city was known for two seasons of weather, primarily summer and autumn.

In summer, temperatures were extremely hot. In autumn, the Santa Ana Winds were prevalent, the leaves turned amber, and buds bloomed into flowers. It did not snow in the winter, and there was occasional rain in the spring.

Many of the rich and famous resided in exclusive areas of Beverly Hills and Hollywood.

Marie became acquainted with talent agent Gordon "Gordy" Macklin. He suggested that she develop a portfolio and follow up with him for possible work.

When Marie contacted Gordy, he linked her to several modeling and acting jobs that required attractive looks and minimal talent. Marie earned good money. She achieved a sense of self-sufficiency and independence. Her self-esteem increased. Her dependency on validation from the opposite sex decreased.

When it appeared that her life was finally on an even keel, Gordy introduced Marie to Ron Davis at a party. Ron had just performed to a sold-out crowd. His career was skyrocketing. He was estranged from his wife, Ebony. Their divorce was pending.

Ron was the former lead singer of the famous R&B vocal group, "The Gems." The group had several platinum-selling albums. When it was time to renegotiate their contract, Ron went solo.

Several months later, Ron's twin brother and former backup singer, Donnell, committed suicide by hanging himself. Ron showed no remorse. He did not attend the funeral, nor did he give his condolences to his sister-in-law, nieces, and nephews. Ron had a reputation for being callous, neurotic, and uncaring.

Ron's smooth talk, good looks, fancy clothes, and fine jewelry mesmerized Marie. In a short time, Marie's nose was wide open. Ron became Marie's idol. She worshipped the ground that he walked on. Marie forfeited her promises to be faithful to God and never commit adultery.

If Marie were alive, she would provide this commentary.

"Life or existing to live day to day is highly exaggerated. My life was cursed from the day I was conceived. My mother died during childbirth. My horny ass father raised me.

The last time I saw Neisha, I confided in her about the drama in my life. I should have left Ron with his wife. Ron convinced me to snort cocaine. I would get so amped up that I snorted heroin and drank alcohol to come down. When I woke up, I was so depressed that I started the binge and crash cycle all over again. God was not pleased with me, and I was going through hell.

Neisha cried and offered to pay the expenses for me to obtain help.

I refused her offer. I told her that Luke 11:26 said something about cleaning your house out, and then the enemy returned with demons seven times stronger than the former ones. The devil must have returned with fourteen demons, seven for Ron and seven for me. I had no intentions of going to a program with dope fiends, drunks, and crack heads.

Neisha stood by me through everything. She kept me on payroll as long as she could. When my drug use became detrimental to my work and put her at risk as my employer, she terminated my employment.

Through it all, I never disclosed to Neisha or anyone else about the extent of the darkness that permeated Ron's life and mine. We were involved in drug dealing, pornography, sexual deviance, and other immoral and ungodly activities. I knew deep inside my soul that there was no coming back. I was angry with myself and mad as hell at the devil. Once again, he used me and laughed at me.

Ron was a heavy, intravenous drug user. If there were a drug that he could inject in his veins, he would use it. On that fateful night, he unsuccessfully tried to locate a vein to inject some heroin. The majority of his veins had collapsed. He was sick from withdrawals and went ballistic.

I didn't try to help him find a vein. I did not want to be bothered. Something in my spirit told me to get up and leave. Instead, I fell into a deep sleep.

At some point, it seemed as though I felt a formidable presence over me. I woke up to find that my left wrist was handcuffed to the bedpost. Ron stood over me with a baseball bat. When I realized his intentions, it was too late. He bludgeoned me with the bat and shot me several times. He wanted me to be graveyard dead.

I gave my pearls to swine, and God turned me over to my reprobate mind. Instead of keeping my promises to God, I responded to an RSVP from hell."

BACK AT JACKSON'S FUNERAL HOME

Dae sat isolated in the rear of *Viewing Room 2* and reflected on the last time that she saw Marie alive. She, Marie, and Neisha were at a famous hotel and spa resort. Neisha paid all expenses for the weekend getaway.

Marie appeared almost skeletal thin. Her usually coiffed hair was in an unevenly cut ponytail. Her beautiful green eyes seemed to have sunk in her eye sockets, and she looked as though she had not slept in months.

While the women relaxed in the Jacuzzi, Dae gulped down her third Margarita. She got all the false courage that she needed to interrogate Marie.

"Hmm, Marie, something tells me that there is a new mystery man in your life."

"Dae, whatever are you talking about? You must be drunk. Boo, you really should lay off that liquor."

Dae licked a small amount of salt from the rim of her glass with the tip of her tongue. Satisfied, she puckered her lips and made a smacking sound.

"Marie, darling, even if I were drunk as you so eloquently put it, I am not stupid. Tell the truth and shame the devil. You only act like a schoolgirl with a crush when a man is involved. You have been missing work and avoiding Neisha and me. On the few recent occasions that I have seen you, your appearance looked like hell, much as it does now. For the record, I am also tired of doing your work. I get paid to do one job, not two."

Neisha laughed.

"Dae, if the truth be told, I think you are overpaid for doing one job."

Dae rolled her eyes at Neisha.

"Ha, ha, Ms. Boss."

Dae refocused her attention on Marie. She began humming the tune from the famous game show, "Jeopardy!"

"Marie, I am still waiting. You have less than five seconds. You can answer in the form of a question if you like."

Marie's face turned scarlet red. She was outraged.

"Dae, you think that you've got jokes. Although it is none of your dam business, Ron and I have reunited. For your nosy ass information, we live together."

Neisha's eyes bulged. She cleared her throat before she spoke.

Neisha asked, "Ron, who?"

Before Marie could answer, Dae interjected.

"Marie, I know that you are not referring to married, no good, asshole Ron."

Marie exclaimed, "Dae, I know that you, of all people, are not judging me. You sleep around with anything that wears pants!"

Dae made a snappy comeback.

"Excuse me, Marie, but I draw the line at married men and dope heads."

Infuriated, Marie replied, "Whatever! Anyway, he is going to divorce that tired ass wife of his. For the record, he is not using drugs, or me."

Neisha intervened. "Ladies, don't you two get started, not here and not now!"

Neisha's eyes drifted towards Marie.

"Honey, no one is judging you. What were you thinking? You have been down that road before and crashed into a wall. It sounds like you are in enough denial for yourself and Ron. When I say denial, I don't mean the river."

Marie shook her head. She kicked at the water with her feet.

"I knew y'all would not understand. That is why I did not tell you. Then again, it is not as though I need anyone's permission. I am a grown ass woman, and it is my life."

Dae replied, "Marie, you are right. I do not understand, nor do I have a clue why you would get back with that fool. However, if it does not work out, Neisha, Bettye, and I will be there to pick up the pieces."

Marie sarcastically stated, "Thank you, but there will not be any broken pieces."

That was the last day that the three of them were together. Dae recalled that she reneged on her promise to support one of her sistahs no matter what. When Marie called, Dae was either too busy or did not want to be bothered. When she did speak to Marie, she was curt and insensitive. She should have been a better friend, a true sistah.

As she stared at the pink casket, Dae remembered a cliché that her granny often quoted.

"But for the grace of God, go I."

Dae's trip down memory lane was abruptly interrupted. She began to cough and perspire profusely. She felt ill.

Dae was HIV positive. Unfortunately, Dae could not fathom how she contracted the often-fatal disease, or to whom she may have transmitted it.

Dae led a pretentious life. She attended Singles' Bible Study on Monday nights and the Pastor's Teaching on Thursday nights. Often, she left the church and went to "The Well," a nightclub approximately 60 miles outside of Los Angeles near Riverside County. She did not want to encounter other sinning saints who partied at the clubs in L.A.

Frequently, Dae sexed young, lustful, thug types that she met at the clubs. However, in her promiscuity, she did not practice safe sex. She dared to think that as an educated Christian woman, she was excluded from the consequences of indulging in sinful behavior.

Dae looked towards the ceiling of the viewing room. With despair in her voice, she questioned aloud, "God, why me?"

Dae realized that Bettye and Neisha overheard her. Embarrassed, she lowered her head, stared at the slightly worn carpet, and attempted to hide the tears that formed in her eyes.

Neisha retreated to her black Mercedes 350 sedan parked in the lot of Jackson's Funeral Home. She began to hyperventilate. She practiced deep breathing exercises. Once her breathing returned to normal, she placed a gospel cassette disc in the compact disc player. She closed her eyes. Her mind drifted back to the day that the police notified her about Marie's murder.

That morning, during breakfast, Neisha expressed her concern about Marie to Barry. She sensed that something was horribly wrong.

"Barry, I have tried to call Marie for a few days. She does not answer her home or cell phone."

"Ne, I am sure that Marie is fine. However, if you are worried, maybe you should go to her house to check on her."

Neisha nodded. She replied, "Yes, I will. I just hate dealing with Ron."

Later that day, as Neisha sat at her desk reviewing the company payroll, her telephone intercom light buzzed. She grabbed the receiver.

Yavette, Neisha's administrative assistant, whispered into the phone. "Ne, two plainclothes detectives are here to see you."

Neisha replied, "That is odd. What do they want?"

Yavette replied, "They didn't say. They asked to see Mrs. Neisha Garrett."

"O.k. Yavette. Please escort them to my office."

The detectives were African American. The taller man stood about six feet two. He probably weighed in on the scales at approximately two hundred and ninety pounds. He wore a dark brown polyester suit. The jacket had one button around his belly. It looked like the button would pop off at any moment.

The shorter man, approximately five feet, eight inches tall, appeared to weigh around one hundred and eighty pounds. He wore a powder blue cotton shirt and navy blue polyester pants that were too short. It looked as though he expected a flood and planned to walk in the rain.

Neisha stifled a laugh. The men reminded her of a black version of the vintage comic strip, "Mutt and Jeff, or detectives Gravedigger and Coffin Ed in the classic movie, "Cotton Comes to Harlem."

She motioned for the detectives to sit in the chairs opposite her meticulously organized desk.

"Hello, gentlemen. How can I possibly be of service to you?"

The taller man made the introductions. He spoke with a slight southern accent.

"Mrs. Garrett, I am Detective Joe Willis. This here is my partner, Detective Reginald Thomas. We are here on official business.

Detective Thomas inquired, "Ma'am, are you acquainted with Marie Danielle Johnson?"

Neisha replied skeptically, "Yes, I am. She is a good friend. But you probably know that because you are here. Is Marie in some sort of trouble?"

Detective Thomas hated being the bearer of bad news, although it was part of his job.

"Mrs. Garrett, I regret to inform you that the bodies of Marie Danielle Johnson and Ronald Davis were discovered in what appears to be a murder-suicide. Mr. Davis left a note."

Neisha's heart did not process what her ears had just heard. Her response came out simultaneously as an inquiry and a scream. She stared at Detective Thomas.

"Is Marie dead?"

"Yes, Mrs. Garrett, it appears so. We need positive identification of her body. She named you as next of kin on several documents. How soon would you be available to meet us at the morgue?"

Between sobs, Neisha stated, "I'll call my husband. We will meet you there within the next hour or so."

"That's fine. We will let ourselves out."

Overwhelmed by grief and shock, Neisha stared at the door.

Yavette inconspicuously peeked out the window. After the detectives exited the parking lot in their unmarked, beat-up brown sedan, she cautiously entered Neisha's office.

Tears streamed down Neisha's face. It was obvious that she was upset.

Yavette asked, "Neisha, what did the detectives want?"

Neisha gasped.

"It appears that Marie is dead. They want me to identify her body."

Yavette exclaimed, "Oh my God!"

Neisha continued. "They believe that Ron murdered her and then killed himself. I have to go to the morgue. Please cancel my appointments. I am taking the rest of the day off. Do not say anything about this to anyone until I confirm that Marie is dead."

"Okay. Neisha, if you need anything, please let me know."

Neisha nodded.

Yavette walked out of the office and gently closed the door. She left Neisha alone to grieve.

Yavette went into the lounge and made a phone call. She disclosed the information about Marie's death to a man on the other end of the phone.

Mortified, Neisha sat at her desk and cried for at least five minutes before she became calm enough to call Barry. She pushed the speed dial button on the phone that connected her directly to Barry's number.

After the fourth ring, he answered, "Hello."

Neisha's voice trembled. "Hi, honey, are you sitting down? I have something important to tell you."

"Ne, you sound upset. It must not be good news."

"Barry, the police just left my office. It appears that Ron murdered Marie and then turned the gun on himself. I have to go to the morgue to identify Marie's body."

"C'mon, Ne. I know that Ron had a few screws loose. Still, it is hard to imagine that he could commit murder and suicide. Are you calm enough to drive?"

"Yes, I'll be fine."

"I'll leave here in ten minutes and meet you there."

"Okay. Barry, I love you."

"I love you more, Neisha."

He hung up.

Neisha recalled the ensuing scenario of her trip to the county morgue. Her eyes scanned the parking lot until she located Barry's silver Range Rover. She parked her car parallel to his. As she walked across the parking lot, she prayed that Marie was alive. She hoped that it was a case of mistaken identity. Deep in her heart, she knew she would never see Marie alive again.

Inside the building, Neisha saw Barry in the lobby looking at the "FBI Most Wanted posters." She walked up behind him and tapped him on his right elbow.

"Hey, baby, let's get this over with."

"Yes, Ne. I don't like this place. Imagine having FBI posters in the lobby of a morgue. Well, I guess the "Most Wanted" have to die too."

Barry and Neisha walked towards Detectives Willis and Thomas, who were engaged in conversation with a uniformed cop.

Neisha introduced them to Barry.

The detectives led Barry and Neisha down a long, narrow hallway. Spider webs dangled from the ceiling. The linoleum floor had large cracks and several mismatched tiles. A horrible stench that resembled mildew, sewage, and antiseptic combined was emitted in the air. At the end of the hallway, they entered a room where hundreds of bodies were concealed in rows and columns of aluminum steel drawers.

In the rear of the room, a petite Asian woman sat behind a desk and observed specimens through a microscope. Her hair was jet black with blue highlights and cut in a Gothic spike hairdo. She wore a white lab coat that resembled an artist's canvas blotted with an abstract finger painting of watercolors. In reality, the colors represented dried up stains of various bodily fluids such as semen, urine, and blood.

When she heard the footsteps, she rose from her desk and approached the foursome. She looked towards Willis and Thomas. She greeted them, "Hello, Detectives."

The men nodded.

Detective Willis stated. "Chin, meet Mr. and Mrs. Garrett."

Chin introduced herself. "Hello, I am Lisa Chin, Assistant County Medical Examiner."

Unresponsive, Neisha stared at her.

Barry spoke for the two of them.

"Hello, Ms. Chin. My wife and I are pleased to meet you."

Chin asked Willis, "Which corpse do you need to identify?"

"Marie Danielle Johnson."

Chin grabbed a pair of latex gloves and cautiously slid them on her hands. She motioned for everyone to follow her. She stopped in front of a column of drawers. Slowly and methodically, she grabbed the handle of drawer number 0915 and pulled it from the wall.

A stained white sheet covered something that resembled the outlining figure of a body. Chin lowered it. Marie's beautiful face was bruised and battered. Black and blue bruises surrounded her left eye from the bludgeoning. Her fine grade of hair was matted with blood. Wooden splinters were lodged in the forehead.

Neisha grabbed Barry's arm.

She screamed, "Oh my God, it is Marie!"

Detective Thomas asked, "Ms. Garrett, can you make an identification of this person?"

"Yes, of course. That is my good friend, Marie Danielle Johnson."

The detective nodded.

"Thank you. Ma'am, we truly apologize that you had to go through this traumatic experience. I understand how you must feel."

"That is one of my best friends lying there. You have no freaking idea how I feel. Sir, I want Marie's body transported from this cold, damp, and mildew smelling morgue to Jackson's Funeral Home as soon as possible."

"Mrs. Garrett, you will need to speak to Chin about the arrangements."

Neisha removed a card from her purse and handed it to Chin.

Neisha implored, "Ms. Chin, I know that you are very busy. Please handle this matter as expeditiously as possible. Feel free to call me any time of day or night."

Chin nodded. She placed the card in her dingy, stained lab coat pocket before replacing the stained sheet over Marie's lifeless body. Chin slowly pushed drawer 0915 into its former position.

Barry and Neisha exited the building.

Over the next few days following Marie's death, Neisha was inconsolable. Pangs of guilt and remorse were so unbearable that she barely ate or slept. She soared in and out of depression. She felt that if she had intervened more, Marie would have left Ron. Perhaps Marie would still be alive.

One evening during dinner, Barry watched as his distraught wife sat at the table and picked at her food.

"Ne, please quit blaming yourself for Marie's death. She had free will and chose to live in darkness. God provided her with a way of escape several times. She forfeited it. You are not God. You do not hold the keys to life or death in your hands. Her time to depart this earth had arrived."

Neisha looked up and stared at Barry.

"I guess so. Barry, do you think she repented in those last few moments before she died? Where do you think she will spend eternal life?"

Before answering, Barry thought briefly about Marie's adultery and drug use. He wondered if she prayed to God and asked for forgiveness with her dying breaths.

Barry shrugged his shoulders. "Ne, do any of us truly know where we will spend eternity?"

She shook her head and continued to pick at her food.

Neisha remained in her car in the parking lot of Jackson's Funeral Home. Memories and nostalgia appeared to consume her thoughts. She clamored for emotional adrenaline. She reminisced about the day that she realized that she was in love with Barry.

As Neisha recalled, she and Dae sat outdoors at a café on Melrose Avenue in West Hollywood. Neisha's pager beeped. She excused herself.

When Neisha returned, Dae immediately gave her unsolicited, yet ongoing, assessment of Barry and Neisha's friendship.

"Ms. Neisha, I'll bet the price of lunch that it was Barry. I keep telling you that the man wants you. It is so obvious that he is in love with you."

Neisha objected. "Whatever."

"Ne, hear me out. Just think for a moment. Barry never likes any of your male friends. He drops everything when you call. In addition, he is one of your major financial, mental, and spiritual supporters. Girl, you better wake up and taste the coffee before some female sips out of your cup. Humph, if I thought the brotha was interested in me, I would be all over him. He is attractive and well off. On the other hand, you are not very cordial to the women that he dates. You never approve of them. You are kind of feeling something for Barry as well."

"Dae, lunch is my treat, so there will not be a coin toss, bet, or anything else. I do not want to hear all that drama. You are incorrigible, 'Ms. I Got to Get Mine.'"

"Neisha, I am just telling it like it t-i-s, tis. There is no need for sarcasm. I am not in the mood for one of your sermons, especially one focused on fornicating or my relationships. Don't hate."

"Dae, I ain't dating or hating. I am waiting on the Lord. I have realized that the more I kissed frogs and hoped that they turned into princes, all I got were warts. No more of that leapfrogging for this sistah. Life ain't a fairy tale, and I ain't Cinderella. On that note, none of those fairy tale characters were Black, even though some of them were wicked as hell."

They laughed.

Neisha continued.

"Anyway, Barry and I are not interested in each other romantically. As far as his paramours, they are usually educated, financially secure, snobby hoochies with no substance. No, I do not approve of them."

"Yes, Neisha, to hear you tell it. I note that you are a little jealous. Here comes our orders. Let's eat, I'm famished."

Between bites of her turkey club sandwich, Neisha wondered who she tried to convince, Dae or herself. The more she thought about it, she realized that she was unsure of her relationship with Barry. Perhaps, God had placed her prince right in front of her face. Soon, she would summon the courage to ask him how he felt about her. Neisha left the café feeling satiated from the meal and with food for thought.

Introducing Barry

Barry Lamont Garrett was born from the union of Florence (Flo) Bradley and Brandon Garrett in New Orleans, Louisiana.

Brandon was Creole. His family's ancestry lineage included Native American, White, Negro, and French blood. He could pass for White. White folks did not accept him because, although he looked White, he was just another colored boy to them. Black folks did not accept him because he could pass for White, so they did not trust him.

Flo's dark skin had a bluish purple tint. She usually wore her thick, coarse black hair in two large plaits that lay midway down her back. Her father was Creole, and her mother was Belizean. When folks labeled her bi-racial, she promptly corrected them in her thick accent.

"Me no bi-nothing. Me mother be one race and me father be anudder one. Dat be equal to two, not bi. If anything, me be two racial."

Barry, the youngest of Brandon and Flo's six children, was the only male child. He was spoiled rotten. He often aggravated his sisters for no reason, especially if he sought attention. They often threatened to throw him in a pit, sell him, or give him to another family, like Joseph's envious brothers in the Bible.

Brandon and Flo went with the children to church every Sunday. After church, the girls assisted Flo in making a huge spread for Sunday dinner. She taught them how to cook, but she also taught them the importance of teamwork. Barry hung out with his father doing "man stuff."

Brandon worked as a porter for the railroad. Brandon died in a train accident after two trains collided on the tracks. Barry was 10 years old.

Flo received a large settlement from the railroad company. She also received Social Security benefits for herself and the children. She placed money in trust funds for each child.

The Garrett household was oblivious to poverty. They did not live lavishly, but they lived well. There was always an abundance of everything. Barry did not know what it was like to be without food, shelter, or wear secondhand clothing.

Despite it all, Barry missed his father. He wanted and needed a male influence in his life. He felt disconnected growing up. Academically, he did well, but there were issues with his attitude. Flo spent a lot of time speaking to the counselors and principals of his schools. A few years after he finished high school, much like the prodigal son, Barry asked for his inheritance.

"Mom, can I have the money from my trust fund?"

Momma Flo responded, "Boy, you must be crazy. No to your foolishness."

Barry knew arguing with his mother was useless, even about his money. He also realized that he would probably squander it if she gave it to him. Nevertheless, he decided to leave Louisiana. He withdrew his money from his personal savings account and purchased a train ticket to Los Angeles. He moved in with his Aunt Katie.

Katie and Flo were as different as night and day. Katie loved to party. She had a lot of Rasta friends and gangsta associates. She introduced Barry to her friends.

Barry's New Orleans country boy persona dissipated as the city man emerged. Barry became involved in racketeering and other illegal activities. He became a recreational drug user.

Barry quickly learned to become a "thug of all trades." His primary job responsibilities were as a bouncer and limousine driver for Carlos. Carlos owned the hottest nightclub in Los Angeles. Barry's additional responsibilities included collecting monies owed to his employer by whatever means necessary, drug dealing, and money laundering. He was a soldier in an army that did not belong to Uncle Sam or God.

Barry also maintained status as a "soldier" during his occasional stints of incarceration. He did not take orders. He gave them. Inside prison, Barry attended church. He did not seek prison religion. He knew God. During services, Barry passed drugs and collected his bounty.

During his last prison sentence, Barry felt a sense of eternal damnation. Death and evil surrounded him. There was no escaping it. He had to shank a few fools to save his ass. If he had to live a square, straight life, he decided that he would never return to prison.

As Barry drove to Jackson's Funeral Home, an oldie but goodie song came on the radio station. A sentimental journey took him back in an emotional time machine to two occasions. The first was when he and Neisha met. The second was when he realized that he was in love with her.

Barry and Neisha became acquainted in a park in South Central Los Angeles frequented by homeless people, drug dealers, and drug users.

Neisha sat alone on a park bench. She did not look like many of the downtrodden and dirty druggies and alcoholics. Yet, she sat there and drank wine from a bottle camouflaged by a brown paper bag.

Several feet away, Barry stood near the basketball court handling his business. He sold large quantities of crack cocaine to dealers at a wholesale rate. That day, business was slow. Bored, he decided to talk to the pretty, chocolate complexion woman who reminded him of his mother. He approached the bench.

"Hello, lady. Do you mind if I sit next to you?"

"It's a public park," she answered flippantly.

Barry liked her spunky attitude. He sat down and introduced himself.

"My name is Barry. I've seen you come through here before."

She raised her right eyebrow and eyed him suspiciously.

"Is that so?"

He nodded.

"My name is Neisha. My friends call me Neisha, Ne, or Ne Ne. My enemies call me crazy."

He laughed.

She lowered the top of the paper bag and revealed a wine bottle.

"Barry, would you like a drink? Don't worry about drinking after me. Alcohol kills germs."

"No thanks. Would you like something to smoke? No strings attached."

"Are you a dirty old man trying to coerce me? Sure, I will take it, but do not get any bright ideas. I am not going to give you anything in exchange."

Barry shook his head.

"Neisha, I do not want to be one of your enemies, so I will not call you crazy. However, you do seem a little eccentric. Here, take this. I don't want anything from you."

He reached inside his waistband and pulled out a package. He handed Neisha a $50 piece of crack cocaine wrapped in cellophane.

She hurriedly grabbed it and hid the package in her bra.

"Wow! Thank you, Barry. Oh, and by the way, don't try to play a sister. I know that eccentric is a fancy way of saying crazy."

"Well, you may be a little eccentric."

They talked about problems that they were experiencing in their respective relationships. There was a kindred type of chemistry between them.

"Neisha, it will take me ten minutes to wrap up my business. Do you wanna hang out? We can get a room, get high, and talk."

"Okay, but no funny business."

Barry crossed his heart.

"Scout's honor. There will be no funny business. Shoot, I might just be a little scared of you."

"Maybe you should be. We eccentric people ain't no joke. We are a force to be reckoned with."

Approximately 10 minutes later, Barry and Neisha left the park. He stopped and bought food on the way to a very nice motel. They did not get high or have sex. They thoroughly enjoyed each other's company.

Barry learned that Neisha did not have any close family. She started smoking crack after her mother died from cancer. She used drugs as a crutch to help deal with depression.

Neisha learned that Barry was raised in a loving family and had a good upbringing. He left New Orleans and journeyed to California to escape the boring country life. He became involved in illegal activities with some ruthless people.

Barry and Neisha became platonic friends who did not experience sexual intimacy. If he or she was romantically involved with someone, that person had to accept his or her friendship. If someone became an enemy of either Barry or Neisha, it became mutual.

After Neisha became saved and sober, she made relentless attempts to persuade Barry to attend church with her. She felt empathetic towards him. He no longer sold or smoked drugs or lived the thug life. But he was unhappy and lacked joy in his life.

Barry eventually decided to accompany Neisha to church. During his first few visits, nothing appeared to soften his heart or touch his soul. However, he noticed that Neisha was full of the Holy Ghost. She spoke in tongues, prayed for people, and appeared to have some sort of anointed power or gift, much like his mother.

On his third visit, the spoken word touched his heart. Barry developed a satiated feeling in his chest. He felt as though it would explode. Tears filled his eyes. One lonely tear escaped his left eye and rolled down his cheek.

Before the end of the service, the preacher made the altar call.

"Is there any man, woman, boy, or girl who wants to accept Jesus Christ and confess Him as Lord and Savior? If anyone wants to receive salvation, please walk towards the altar."

Barry stood up.

Neisha escorted him to the altar.

Neisha waited in the foyer for Barry. She commended him on his decision to accept salvation. She cried tears of joy.

Barry invited her to dine with him at "The Skipper's Table," a restaurant in Marina Del Rey, an upscale beach community. He felt that she could empathize with his current state of emotional, mental, and spiritual upheaval. He was sick and tired of being sick and tired.

Barry arrived at the restaurant before Neisha. He hung his navy blue suit jacket on the hook in the rear of his black Lexus sedan. He removed his gray silk tie with the diamond tie clip and placed the items in the glove compartment. Barry reclined back in his seat and listened to his favorite jazz station.

Neisha's arrival interrupted Barry's meditation. Her car had a unique sputtering, kaboom, chug-a-lug sound that could be distinguished blocks away. Barry offered to finance a car for her or, at the very least, give her one of his. She declined. Her prideful self chose to ride around town in "Betsy the Bucket."

The twosome exited their respective cars and walked down the boardwalk to the restaurant. They paused to observe two seagulls screech loudly as the hungry birds fought over a piece of fish. The bird with the largest portion eventually snatched the tail end of the fish from the other bird and swiftly flew away. The foodless bird took off in pursuit and screeched loudly, "Ag, ag, ag."

Barry and Neisha laughed.

"Barry, those birds remind me of your people. Why didn't they share?"

He chuckled.

"You mean your people, Black folks."

Neisha frowned.

"Yeah, God's and mine. I always say that God has a sense of humor, which is why He created us. There is never a dull moment. We are a peculiar people."

"Ne, you got that right."

As they resumed walking, they looked at the glamorous and expensive boats docked on the bluish green, still water.

Neisha thought, "One day, I will be able to afford to live like this."

The restaurant was crowded. A large aquarium, with beautifully colored tropical fish, was located near the entrance of the waiting area. Seashells and artificial coral reefs hung on the walls to complement the beach-like decor. People clustered around as they waited for seating to become available.

Barry approached the greeter, an attractive, young White woman named Heather. Blonde highlights accentuated her shoulder-length, brunette hair. She had a large bosom, small waist, and flat buttocks.

Barry asked, "Heather, can we have a rear booth?"

Heather smiled at Barry and winked. She rolled her eyes at Neisha. She spoke with a valley girl accent.

"Sure, Barry-O, anything for you."

On her notepad, she wrote, Barry 2.

Heather walked away.

Neisha whispered to Barry, "Humph, that stupid white girl doesn't know me like that to be rolling her eyes at me. You need to check her butt and put her in place."

"Ne, remember that you just left church."

"Yes, that's why I didn't nut up on her."

Barry shook his head. "You are incorrigible."

Neisha ignored him. She gazed at the autographed 8" x 10" glossy pictures of celebrities posted on the walls.

Several minutes later, Heather returned. She summoned Barry and Neisha to a secluded booth in the rear section of the restaurant.

Barry and Neisha sat across from each other. They were separated by a table covered with a red and white checkered, linen tablecloth. Silverware, wrapped in red cloth napkins, lay on the table in front of them. A crystal vase held one single red rose with leaves of pink and white baby's breath. Dim light emitted from a candle strategically positioned in the center of the table. Contemporary jazz music filtered softly through speakers.

An extremely attractive white male server named Sean brought their menus. He directed his inquiry to Barry.

"Sir, are you ready to order or do you need more time to look at the menu?"

Barry shook his head. "Please give us a few minutes."

Sean replied, "Yes, sir."

As Sean walked away, Neisha's eyes followed him.

"That is a fine White dude. I bet that he makes more tips than Heathen, Heifer, Heather, or whatever her dang name is."

Barry imitated Neisha, "Humph."

Neisha gazed at the prices on the menu and gasped. "Wow!"

Barry whispered, "Ne, order whatever your stomach desires. Money is no object."

Neisha gave Barry her order. She continued to scrutinize her surroundings.

"Barry, I am impressed with the ambiance of this place. Who do you bring here, business partners or the superficial women that you date?"

Barry frowned.

"Superficial? See, that is why I nicknamed you Nosy Neisha. I refuse to answer on the grounds of self-incrimination."

"Barry, sometimes, you can be such a smart aleck. For your info, Nosy is spelled K-n-o-w-s-y because I like to "knows why.""

She stuck her tongue out at him.

He shook his head, tilted it to the side, and grinned. Then, feeling convicted, yet liberated, from his earlier experiences at church, Barry leaned over the table. He spoke softly and shared secrets with Neisha that he never mentioned to a living soul.

Neisha listened attentively. She looked deep into his eyes as he spoke. It was as if her eyes pierced the inner depths of his soul.

As if on cue, Sean returned at that moment.

Barry seized the opportunity to dismiss the feelings stirring inside of him.

"Sean, I will have the Ribeye Steak Dinner with All-U-Can-Eat Shrimp. I would like my steak cooked medium well. For side orders, I will have onion rings and steamed vegetables. My companion will have the Filet Mignon Dinner, steak well done, baked potato with butter, and steamed broccoli. We will each have lemonade and tossed green salads with ranch dressing while we wait."

Sean retrieved the menus. "Thank you. I'll return shortly with your drinks and salads."

Neisha laughed. "Ooh, today I am your companion."

The food was delicious, and the service was excellent. Neisha ate until she could not pass one morsel of food through her lips. She ordered a slice of pineapple coconut cake to go.

Barry and Neisha left the restaurant and walked along the beach. She carried her church pumps in one hand and walked barefoot in the sand.

In a remote area, they sat on a huge, grey slate boulder and watched as the sun methodically began to disappear from the sky. A large, reddish-orange tint flamed over the bluish green, still water. The scene was romantically breathtaking.

At that very moment, Barry could no longer deny that he was in love with Neisha. Earlier that day, he poured out his soul to her. He decided not to share his feelings. Their friendship had withstood many trials and hardships. The thought of rejection was more than he wanted to consider. He realized that the other women in his life were mere substitutes. Perhaps that was why his relationships failed.

Barry wanted to spend more time with Neisha.

"Ne, let's take a boat ride."

Neisha imitated Heather.

"Okay, Barry-O, anything for you."

He frowned.

"Let it go, Neisha. Mockery doesn't become you."

"Aw, I thought it was a good impression."

"Let me help you with your shoes so we can get to the docks before it is too late."

Barry and Neisha boarded a blue and white mariner boat named *Daisy's Dream*. An elderly White couple sat opposite them.

The woman appeared to have her eyes fixated on Neisha and Barry.

Neisha felt uncomfortable. She squirmed in her seat.

Finally, after several moments passed, the woman grinned. She grabbed her husband's hand and held it tight.

The woman stated, "Sweetheart, don't they remind you of us at that age? We were so in love and without a care in the world. Hell, we still are."

Her husband nodded in agreement and squeezed her hand.

Barry and Neisha smiled.

Neisha leaned her head on Barry's shoulder.

After the boat ride, Barry escorted Neisha to her car. He kissed her cheek and watched as she drove off in Betsy the Bucket.

As he drove home, Barry let out a huge sigh. It had been quite a day. That night, he kneeled beside his bed and sincerely prayed with a repentant heart. He was ready to give his life to the Lord and his heart to Neisha if she would accept it. His mother would be ecstatic.

Later that year, after they dined in the Marina, Neisha and Barry were alone in her office. The annual Christmas Holiday Outreach Event hosted by her nonprofit organization had concluded.

Neisha retrieved two sodas from the mini refrigerator underneath her desk. She sat next to Barry on the sofa.

"Whew! Barry, this year's crowd was the largest ever. Did you see the cute little boy who followed me around? He told me that he was Blexian, half Black and half Mexican."

"Yes, Ne, it was a huge turnout. I am exhausted. I saw little dude on your tail. He was smitten with you. He has good taste."

Neisha felt that it was the appropriate time to inquire about Barry's feelings for her.

Neisha asked bluntly. "Barry, are you in love with me?"

The unexpected question caught him off guard. He avoided eye contact with Neisha and tried to laugh it off.

"What? Neisha, you are so crazy."

"I may be crazy, eccentric, or whatever you want to call it, but you are not leaving here without answering me."

Neisha removed Barry's purple and gold Lakers cap from the backwards position on his head and placed it on the table. She reached for Barry's left hand and placed it gently in hers.

Barry sweated bullets of perspiration.

Neisha looked lovingly into his eyes.

"Barry, I am still waiting for an answer."

80

He realized that she was serious.

Barry stammered nervously, "Neisha, you, uh, uh, know I can't lie to you. Yes, I have loved you for years. I realized that I was in love with you when we spent the day in the Marina. I would love to spend the rest of my life with you."

Barry felt relieved that his love for Neisha was finally out in the open. He had no idea where her inquisition was leading. He anxiously waited for her to continue.

Neisha moved closer to him.

"Barry, the feeling is mutual. I am in love with you as well. I would love for us to spend the rest of our lives together."

Barry held on to Neisha's hand as he kneeled on one knee.

"Neisha Lynette Fuller, would you be my wife?"

"Yes, of course. But let us get a couple of things straight. I want a respectable courtship. You are not getting any nooky until we are married. We will attend premarital counseling. You know that I am not very domesticated. I don't have a passion for cooking, dusting, and cleaning, but I will work on it."

He sat next to Neisha.

"Whew! Our engagement will be official when I put a ring on your beautiful finger. We'll go shopping tomorrow."

Neisha proclaimed, "By the way, we will get tested for sexually transmitted diseases before making an appointment for premarital counseling. I know some of those scags and scallywags that you dated. And, you know some of those scrubs and thugs that I dated! Go through your little black book or wherever you keep your numbers and let those females know that you are no longer eligible or single. Drop 'em like they're hot."

"Ne, where did a Christian woman and missionary learn that kind of language? Never mind, do not answer. If the truth be told, your versatility and genuineness are only a few of the many things that I love about you."

She laughed. "God loves me and my versatility."

He embraced her. Their lips met. They engaged in a long, passionate kiss. It sealed their commitment to each other. The body temperature in the room turned up.

Neisha felt like putty in his arms.

Barry looked deep into her big brown eyes.

"I love you, Neisha Lynette Fuller."

"I love you, too, Barry Lamont Garrett."

They kissed again, passionately.

Barry gasped. His heartbeat increased profusely. He stepped away as a bulge began to develop near his groin.

"Neisha, I think we need to go home to our separate dwellings before something starts that we cannot finish."

She agreed.

B arry is very attractive. His head is clean-shaven like the actors who starred as the cop, Kojak". He has broad shoulders and thick muscles. When he wears a suit, he looks like a Black Adonis. His beard and moustache are always impeccably trimmed. Barry's manicured nails camouflage any evidence of former hard labor or deviant behavior. His only flaw, if you would call it that, is the slight pudginess in his mid-section. Nevertheless, he carries his weight with authority. Built like a professional athlete, his physical appearance often intimidates people.

A redeemed Elder Barry Garrett oversees the youth ministry of the church. He works with at-risk young men, mostly African American and Latino, between the ages of 12-17 years old. In addition, Barry owns a for-profit consulting firm. He and his friend, Russell, are co-owners of a limousine business. His income nets well over $250,000 per year.

There are some things that Barry just has no tolerance for, which include challenging his faith or messing with his family or money. Someone was agonizing Neisha. Barry was determined to get to the bottom of it.

Neisha looked at the expensive designer watch on her wrist. More than twenty minutes had passed since she retreated to her car in the lot of Jackson's Funeral Home. She needed to return inside. She hoped that Dae had sobered up, or at the very least decided to shut up with her nonsense.

Before she exited the car, Neisha prayed.

"Lord, please help me to be humble, vigilant, and focused. You know my heart, and you know how desperately I wanted to slap the taste of liquor out of Dae's mouth."

Neisha gathered her things, locked the car, and proceeded back towards the funeral home. She was unaware that someone watched her from a distance.

Neisha retreated to *Viewing Room 2* and informed Dae and Bettye that she was going to the chapel.

In the chapel, Neisha prayed and cried before the altar. Suddenly, brisk, cool air seemed to fill the room. She felt an eerie chill in her body and a feeling of a demonic presence. She saw a vision of her former friend, Jeannine. The woman dangled a knife in one hand and a noose in the other. Sounds of hideous laughter crept from her mouth.

Neisha shuddered. She had not been in contact with Jeannine ever since Jeannine was committed to an institution for the criminally insane several years ago.

When Barry arrived at Jackson's Funeral Home, Myisha was not seated in the lobby. He checked the directory for Marie's name. He proceeded to *Viewing Room 2*.

Bettye and Dae were engaged in conversation with a few of Marie's friends. Neisha was nowhere in sight.

After the conversation ended, Barry approached Bettye and Dae.

"Hi ladies, where is Neisha?"

Bettye hugged him.

"Hi Barry, she's in the chapel. She will be glad to see you. She is pretty torn up."

"Thanks, Bettye. I'll go find her."

Dae's greeting was flat.

"Hello."

Aware of Dae's impeccable capability to make bad situations even worse, Barry asked, "Dae, is there any reason that my wife is upset other than grieving for her friend?"

Dae shrugged her shoulders and rolled her eyes.

"It beats the hell out of me."

Barry walked away.

The chapel was located to the right of the entrance of the funeral home. Barry watched from a distance as Neisha kneeled at the altar, praying.

A woman walked through the lobby. She bumped into Barry as she passed by. She wore dark glasses. A large Sunday church hat covered the crown of her head and forehead.

From the brief glimpse of the woman, Barry was certain that he recognized her from somewhere. She resembled Niesha's former friend, Jeannine. The woman was the same height, but at least one hundred pounds smaller than Jeannine. Yet, something about the woman disturbed Barry's spirit.

Barry rushed out of the building to get a better glimpse of her. As he stepped onto the asphalt of the parking lot, someone drove a speeding car in his direction. He leaped out of the car's path just in time.

The mysterious woman was behind the steering wheel of the car. It appeared as though she deliberately tried to run him down.

Barry muttered, "Oh hell no."

Stunned and bewildered, Barry rushed inside the funeral home to check on Neisha. When he entered, he found her in the same position at the altar. He kneeled and embraced her.

Neisha grabbed his hand.

"Hi, baby. I am so glad that you're here."

"How are you holding up, Ne?"

Tears filled her eyes.

"Dae was under the influence when I arrived. She decided to comb Marie's wig, and it flew off, revealing all those ugly scars. I nearly had a panic attack. To top it off, I just had a vision that Jeannine tried to strangle me."

He decided not to tell Neisha about the mysterious woman.

"Ne, it's been a long day. Let's go home."

She nodded.

Barry and Neisha returned to *Viewing Room 2* and informed Bettye and Dae that they were leaving.

Neisha stopped at the area outside the viewing room and perused the guestbook. On the last page, someone scribbled in red ink, "I'll get you, Neisha."

Neisha gasped.

Barry snatched the page from the book. He escorted Neisha to her car.

Barry became concerned that the two incidents regarding the car and the guestbook were not coincidences. The mysterious woman may have been stalking Neisha at the funeral home. She could be responsible for the harassing phone calls.

Bettye left Jackson's Funeral Home approximately ten minutes after Barry and Neisha departed. As she drove to her five-star hotel, she was perplexed. David did not respond to any of her messages. The experience at the funeral home, and the calls from Janice left her emotionally, spiritually, and physically exhausted.

Once she arrived at the hotel. Betty was anxious to take a hot shower and store the day's events in her brain's hard drive. She exited the elevator and walked swiftly to her suite. She slid the white plastic key card in the slot on the door. When the indicator light flashed green, she turned the door handle and entered the room.

Fear crept through her body as she thought she heard a noise coming from the bedroom. She sensed a presence coming from the closet area. Bettye grabbed the base of the lamp in case she needed a weapon.

Suddenly, David lunged from behind the closet door. Water dripped from his upper chest. He wore a large bath towel around his waist.

David yelled, "Surprise!"

Bettye dropped the lamp. It broke into pieces.

"David, are you crazy? You nearly gave me a heart attack. You are going to pay for this lamp."

"Yes, Bettye, I'm crazy about you. I came early. I thought you could use some company. Come here, woman, and kiss me."

Bettye snatched the towel from his waist and pushed him onto the bed.

Introducing David

David Butler was born in Mobile, Alabama. At the age of eight, he was sent to Atlanta, Georgia, to live with his maternal grandparents. His younger sister and brother remained at home with their parents. To this day, David does not understand why he was estranged from his parents.

David's mother, Susan, is a chemist. His father, Daniel, is a psychiatrist. David's parents are atheists. They do not believe in a divine creator. Their beliefs are more in alignment with the Big Bang theory. David's father believes that if there were a God, his family would not have endured many of the atrocities that occurred in their lives. His parents detest his belief in God.

David's paternal grandfather is currently serving life in prison without the possibility of parole for murdering David's grandmother.

David's brother and sister are musicians with a famous heavy metal rock band. Both are addicted to drugs. His sister has nearly died on several occasions from overdoses. His brother is gay. Neither of them particularly cares for David nor his straight-laced lifestyle.

David is intelligent, rich, and handsome. His blue eyes are comparable to the sky on a clear day or the deep blue sea, beautiful and tranquil. His hair is jet black like unadulterated coal.

In addition to being the pastor of one of the largest congregations in Atlanta, Georgia, David is a licensed clinical psychologist with a lucrative private practice. He specializes in forensic psychology. He is the author of several bestselling books.

David's parents vowed to disown him several times because of his religious beliefs. They grew tired of hearing him talk about God, salvation, deliverance, and sin. They ultimately forbade him from discussing that nonsense in their home.

After David married Bettye, his parents considered it the ultimate betrayal. They felt disgraced and humiliated. Bettye and her children were not welcome in their home. Therefore, David chose not to visit them. David has not communicated with his parents and siblings in several years.

When Barry and Neisha became engaged, the first person that Neisha informed was Ms. Jenna. The phone rang five times before the answering machine picked up. At the sound of Neisha's voice, Ms. Jenna answered the phone.

"Hi, Ms. Jenna. How are you?

"I am fine. How are you? You sound out of breath, excited."

"You know me much too well. I need your help to plan my wedding. Barry and I are engaged."

"Congratulations, Neisha, but I am not surprised. Everyone could see that the two of you were in love. I do not know why it took you so long to realize it. I will cover all your expenses for the wedding. Don't worry about anything."

Neisha was elated. She did not know how she would pay for a wedding. She knew that if she refused Ms. Jenna's generous offer that Ms. Jenna would be insulted.

"Thanks, Ms. Jenna. I haven't thought about expenses. I thought it would probably be a small informal gathering. Are you sure?"

"Neisha, we are going to spare no expenses. I know that you're busy, so we'll talk later. We have a lot of planning to do. Congratulations, and give my love to Barry."

Neisha ended the conversation by stating, "I appreciate and love you so much."

After dinner that evening, Neisha telephoned Bettye to share her good news.

When Bettye heard Neisha's voice, she prayed things were well. It was 10 p.m. in Atlanta. Neisha rarely called that late.

"Hi Neisha. Girl, what's happening?"

"Not a whole lot. I just had to share my good news with you. This is my first real break today. Barry and I are getting married."

"Hold on, Neisha. Let me clean the wax out of my ears. Dang, you can't find a cu-tip or bobby pin when you need one."

Neisha laughed.

"Stop playing, Bettye. You heard me. I finally got the courage to ask Barry how he felt about me, and he confessed. I took it from there."

"You know that I am sincerely happy for you. David must have known earlier. That is why he asked me several times if I had spoken to you. I will deal with him later."

"Bettye, I want you to be one of my bridesmaids. Also, if it is okay with you, I would like David to give me away."

"Neisha, name the time and place. I will be one of your bridesmaids. David will be honored. You know he considers himself as the white sheep of the family."

They laughed.

Bettye changed the subject.

"Ne, give me the inside scoop. I know you haven't been keeping s-e-x secrets from me."

"Bettye, you know I am celibate. There will be no hanky panky until Barry and I are married."

Bettye laughed.

"Ne, don't nobody say hanky panky anymore."

Neisha retorted, "I just did. Better yet, there will be no hanky, no panky, and definitely no stanky."

"Ne, you are crazy, so crazy, and more than a lil crazy."

They chuckled and said their goodbyes.

The following day, Neisha telephoned Dae, Marie, and Jeannine to share the good news about her engagement. Not one of them seemed happy for her.

Dae reluctantly agreed to be a bridesmaid.

Marie said she was not fond of weddings but agreed to be there for Neisha.

Jeannine responded. "Neisha, I am sure I will be busy that day."

Puzzled, Neisha asked, "Jeannine, how do you know you will be busy since the date has not been set?"

"I just will, Neisha. Goodbye."

Jeannine hung up without allowing Neisha further opportunity to speak.

Neisha's feelings were hurt. She remembered that people are in your life for a reason, season, or lifetime. She also realized that she needed to quit trying to make seasonal people, lifetime folks. God repeatedly revealed to her that Jeannine's season was up.

Neisha concluded that it would be the last time that she allowed Jeannine to hurt her feelings.

Neisha was true to her word. She remained celibate during her and Barry's courtship. It was not easy. Many nights after she and Barry went out, she returned home and took a cold shower or a long, hot bath. She prayed to God for strength and endurance.

The engaged couple received marriage counseling as agreed. After several sessions, their pastor gave them his blessing. He could not find any reason why they should not get married.

Their tests for sexually transmitted diseases were negative.

After Barry shared his results with Neisha, he asked, "If any of my test results were positive, would you still marry me?"

She looked at him seriously without cracking a smile.

"Don't be silly, of course I would."

Ms. Jenna and Neisha shopped for bridesmaids' dresses in the garment district, also known as *The Alley* in downtown Los Angeles. Consumers can purchase clothing, accessories, and other items at discounted and wholesale prices. Everything from fake eyelashes, Air Jordans, alligator shoes, or wedding gowns is for sale. Some of the drawbacks to shopping in *The Alley* are that so-called designer items are sometimes counterfeit, parking is expensive, items are rarely tagged, and vendors randomly select what prices they want to charge customers. The large crowds of people can also be overwhelming,

Ms. Jenna and Neisha entered a retail store that specialized in formals, gowns, and bridal wear. They selected a beautiful ivory dress for the bridesmaids.

Neisha looked at the price tag and gasped.

Ms. Jenna looked at the price tag. She did not flinch.

A woman with a deep Latin accent approached them.

She inquired, "May I help you, ladies?"

Ms. Jenna replied, "I would like to speak to the owner."

The woman asked, "Ma'am, are you sure I cannot help you?"

In a polite but firm tone, Ms. Jenna replied, "Yes, I am sure."

The woman called out, "Sonny."

A man entered from the rear of the store. As he opened the door, a pungent aroma of curry food filled the air. He sucked a piece of food from his smoke-stained teeth. He walked with a slight limp in his right leg.

The woman pointed to Ms. Jenna.

"She asked to speak to the owner."

Sonny looked at Jenna suspiciously.

"Hello, I am Sonny, the owner."

"It is a pleasure to meet you, Sonny. My name is Jenna. I am interested in purchasing eight of these dresses. I have a list of sizes. Would you be able to accommodate me, at a discounted price, of course?"

Sonny repeated the quantity. "Ma'am, did you say eight?"

"Yes, I did. The dresses are for Neisha's bridesmaids."

Ms. Jenna pointed to Neisha, who was still browsing around the store.

"Of course, I can fill your order. I will also give you a ten percent discount."

"I will pay for the dresses today. I would like a twenty percent discount."

Ms. Jenna and Sonny settled on a fifteen percent discount and free alterations. Ms. Jenna gave Sonny a personal check and her identification.

Sonny excused himself to make a telephone call to the bank.

Ms. Jenna walked over to Neisha and laughed.

"He thinks my check won't clear. Watch and learn."

Sonny's demeanor improved after the check was approved. He smiled like a Cheshire cat. He no longer treated them as a couple of Black women who were simply window-shopping.

As they prepared to leave, Ms. Jenna extended her right hand.

Sonny eagerly shook her hand.

"Thank you so much. Here is my card. Please tell your friends. I will personally call you when your order is ready."

Outside the store, Neisha cried. "Thank you, Ms. Jenna. What would I do without you?"

Ms. Jenna smiled.

"Neisha, let's grab something to eat before we go to the westside for your dress. I'll purchase mine later."

"Okay, Ms. Jenna. I thought we were going to shop for my dress here in The Alley. You can't keep spending money on my wedding like it is water."

"Neisha, don't worry. You are the daughter that I never had. God has blessed me. This is not a financial burden."

After lunch, Ms. Jenna drove to a bridal shop that sold the most exquisite clothing Neisha could imagine. Several dresses were trimmed with mink or pearls. A dress accentuated with diamonds was securely locked in a glass showcase.

Ms. Jenna picked an ivory colored lace dress with a pearl neckline. The train was decorated with white and black pearls.

"Neisha, this dress is perfect for you."

Neisha stated, "That dress has my name written all over it."

Neisha tried on the dress.

"Neisha, you look beautiful. You won't be able to gain too many pounds before the wedding."

Neisha nodded her head in agreement.

Ms. Jenna paid for the dress with her American Express Card. She handed the dress to Neisha.

"You better not start blubbering."

Ms. Jenna lived in a large home in the exclusive Hancock Park area of Los Angeles. Historically, Negroes were not allowed to buy homes in the area. The great singer, actor ,and musician, Nat King Cole was one of the first, if not the first to integrate the neighborhood.

Neisha had only seen homes like Ms. Jenna's in magazines. The first time that she visited Ms. Jenna's home, she wondered how Ms. Jenna could afford the home and many of the expensive belongings that she possessed. It was short of being considered a mansion.

Neisha, nosy as she admitted to being, would never have asked Ms. Jenna about her finances. Neisha concluded that several things seemed obscure and did not add up. There was more to Ms. Jenna than teaching and church involvement.

On a Saturday evening, a few weeks before the wedding, Neisha and Ms. Jenna were at Ms. Jenna's home preparing food for Sunday dinner.

Neisha stood near the sink, peeling, and dicing potatoes for Cajun-style potato salad.

Several feet away, Ms. Jenna stood at the stove, lowering the heat under the pot of curly mustard greens with fatback. Sensing that Neisha was in a solemn mood, she turned and looked at her.

"Baby, what's on your mind? You seem burdened, troubled."

"Ms. Jenna, I will marry a wonderful man in a few weeks. You have been so supportive. Aside from the financial help, you have been helping me with things that any woman my age should know, such as cooking and cleaning. I am grateful."

Neisha laid down the knife. She paused for several seconds and then continued.

"To be quite honest, I am worried about my wedding night. I do not know what it is like for a saved, Christian woman to make love with her saved, Christian husband. I do not want to be a prude, but I do not want to be too freaky. I know this all sounds insane. Heck, should I enjoy making love to my husband or lie there and do it missionary style? Making noise would probably be inappropriate. What do Christian couples do? I see some couples at church and cannot imagine them doing anything together in bed. If so, I figure that they do it, roll over, and go to sleep. I am not trying to get down like that."

Ms. Jenna laughed so hard that she cried. Once she gained her composure, she walked over to Neisha and grabbed her hand.

"Neisha, baby, Barry will be your husband. Of course, it is okay to enjoy making love with him. Neither of you are virgins. That man loves you so much. Just let him lead you, and things will be okay. Buy some sexy lingerie, wear an expensive, soft fragrance, turn on romantic music, and let him make his move. Please do not lie there all stiff like an ironing board. I sure enjoyed my Andrew. It's been over forty years, but I still remember."

Neisha kissed Ms. Jenna on the cheek.

"Thank God for you, Ms. Jenna. I love you so much. Barry and I will name our first daughter after you."

"Okay, but don't be surprised if that child grows up to resent you forgiving her that antiquated name. I love you too, Neisha. Now, enough of this sentiment. Please make the potato salad and watch those greens for me. I am going to take a nap. We'll fry the chicken tomorrow after church."

A few years after Neisha and Barry were married, Ms. Jenna complained of blurred vision, headaches, and nausea. Neisha insisted on taking her to the doctor. Ms. Jenna was diagnosed with a cancerous, inoperable brain tumor. Doctors gave her three months to live. Contrary to their report, she remained alive for more than a year. Neisha and Barry were there for her day and night.

When Ms. Jenna began receiving hospice services, she gave Neisha an envelope with strict instructions to open it immediately after she died.

Neisha opened the envelope the following day after Ms. Jenna passed. Inside were instructions for the funeral, an insurance policy, and a business card for an attorney. The insurance policy, worth $250,000, named Neisha Lynette Fuller-Garrett as the beneficiary. Neisha was astounded. There were further instructions for Neisha to contact Ms. Jenna's attorney.

In a respectable amount of time, after the funeral, Neisha contacted Ms. Jenna's attorney. They scheduled an appointment for the reading of Ms. Jenna's will.

Jefferson Jordan, Attorney-at-Law, was an attractive African American male approximately five feet, nine inches tall. He wore his hair in shoulder length dreadlocks. On his right wrist, he donned a paved chocolate and white diamond watch. He sported a matching ring on his right ring finger.

Barry and Neisha met with Mr. Jordan in his plush penthouse office located in Beverly Hills. Several plaques, degrees, and awards hung on the wall.

After the threesome dispensed with introductions and pleasantries, Mr. Jordan stated, "Jenna Brown-Porter was a very wealthy woman. She was the daughter of scientist and inventor Franklin Brown and the daughter-in-law of businessman Israel Porter. After her husband, Andrew, died, she inherited the entire Porter estate, which was massive. At that time, the Porters were the wealthiest Black people in America. She later inherited her parents' estate. She held the rights to her father's patents on products that were never released. Those patents, if ever developed, could be worth a fortune."

Neisha looked puzzled.

"Mr. Jordan, did you have me come to Beverly Hills for a history lesson?"

He laughed.

"Certainly not. Neisha, as you know, Jenna did not have any immediate family. You were like a daughter to her. Jenna bequeathed almost everything that she owned to you, both money and real property. Her estate is valued at more than $25,000,000. You are named as the beneficiary of a savings account with a balance of $5,000,000. You have immediate access to that account. All the legal documents are in the briefcase."

He slid a leather briefcase in front of her.

Neisha gasped.

"Mr. Jordan, let me get this right. Are you telling me that I am a millionaire?"

He laughed again.

"Everyone calls me J.J. Yes, you are an extremely wealthy woman. Please look at the documents."

"J.J., I am overwhelmed. I am not interested in reviewing the paperwork right now. I need to digest this and discuss it with my husband. Is it possible to retain you as my attorney? If Ms. Jenna trusted you, so do I."

"Neisha, there are several documents that need your signature acknowledging this meeting, and that you received the paperwork. It would be my pleasure to be your attorney. I worked with Jenna for many years. I started with this firm doing clerical work. She paid for me to go to law school. Keep the briefcase, it is yours. That is how we do it in Beverly Hills. Give me a call next week, and we will set up an appointment. I will walk you and Barry to the lobby."

Barry and Neisha stood at the elevator. He was astounded. She was in shock.

"Neisha, did you have any idea that Ms. Jenna was married to Andrew Porter? His family is a legacy in Black History. Her father also made significant contributions. He was a well-known scientist and inventor."

Neisha shook her head. "No idea whatsoever. This course of events might change our lives a little.

Barry laughed. "Yeah, wifey, maybe just a little ."

Neisha thought about purchasing a small boat and docking it at Marina Del Rey.

After Neisha received her inheritance, she and Barry leased the home in View Park. They paid cash for a home in Ladera Heights. Their home is located on a quiet cul-de-sac near Slauson Avenue and La Cienega Boulevard. The least expensive homes in that area have an estimated value of $500,000. Their home is valued at over $750,000.

Barry and Neisha's home fulfills all their needs. It has a spacious living room with a fireplace, five bedrooms, three full baths, plenty of closet space, a dining area, a large kitchen, and a den. Attached to the house is a two-car garage. A circular driveway separates the professionally landscaped front lawn from the entrance to the home.

After the viewing at Jackson's Funeral Home earlier that day, Neisha was anxious to cross the threshold of the comfort and peace of home. She sought refuge on the sofa. She fell asleep shortly after she sat down.

Barry had not eaten all day. His stomach growled like a bear coming out of hibernation. He went into the kitchen and made a hefty sandwich from the leftover roast beef in the fridge.

After he compensated his stomach with food, Barry telephoned *DE JA BOO Flowers and Gifts* in Ladera Heights. He ordered two dozen each of yellow and red roses for delivery. Barry went upstairs and ran Neisha's bathwater. When he returned downstairs, she remained asleep on the sofa.

Barry shook her gently.

"Ne, baby, I ran your bath water. Get ready for bed."

107

After a long, hot bath, Neisha entered the bedroom and noticed a trail of rose petals from the bathroom door to their bed. Her husband's compassion and sensitivity moved her deeply. Only God deserved the glory for the change in Barry's life.

After Barry finished his shower, they knelt beside the bed and prayed. Once in bed, they made passionate love. They fell asleep wrapped in each other's arms.

Barry woke up a few hours later. He went downstairs to the kitchen. As he sat at the table eating the remainder of the roast beef sandwich, he wrestled with his decision not to tell Neisha about the mysterious woman.

The following day, a disturbed Barry gazed at the pictures of him and Neisha on his desk. His eyes glanced over their wedding picture.

In the past, it had never occurred to him that he and Neisha would find love with each other. He was usually involved with some clingy woman who wanted the white picket fence life. At that time, the last thing on his mind was settling down. On the other hand, it seemed that Neisha attracted the psychotic, stalker types, who were possessive, obsessive, and assaultive.

Despite it all, and unbeknownst to them, God had a plan for their lives. They had seen each other at their worst. It seemed fitting that God would allow them to be together in better times.

Barry is in love with his saved, crazy, and sanctified wife. With all that is within his power, he is not going to allow anyone to harm her or jeopardize the sanctity of their marriage.

When Neisha began receiving the harassing phone calls, Barry and Neisha developed a list of possible suspects. Ironically, Dae's name was on the list.

Barry made it no secret that he did not like Dae. As far as he was concerned, she was selfish and egotistical. Dae did not only have issues, but she had a subscription to Misery Magazine.

Barry recalled the night that Dae tried to seduce him.

Dae telephoned Barry at his office with the pretense that Neisha needed him to stop by after work. She claimed that Neisha was in a meeting and asked her to make the call.

When Barry arrived, Neisha's car was not in the parking lot. He used his key to gain entrance into the building and went directly to Neisha's office. He opened the door.

Dae stood by the desk.

Barry became perturbed.

"Dae, where is Neisha?"

"She's not here. It is only you and me."

Dae approached Barry and stood within a few feet of him. She tossed the short, one-piece dress over her shoulders and revealed a sexy, expensive negligee.

"You know how desperately I want you. I know that you want me too."

Barry grabbed her shoulders.

"Dae, have you completely lost your mind? The feeling is definitely not mutual. Through the years, I have repeatedly told Neisha that you were a snake. This proves it."

Barry stormed out, slamming the door behind him.

Barry immediately informed Neisha of her wicked friend's deceitful ploy. He was disturbed by Neisha's nonchalant attitude.

She simply stated, "I'll deal with it at the right time and the right place. My mother used to tell me to keep my enemies close and my so-called frenemies even closer."

Ronald Davis was also considered a prime suspect for the harassment and threats. Ronald and Neisha had a mutual dislike for each other. Neisha made it emphatically clear that she did not approve of Marie's relationship with him. However, he was currently not a threat. His soul was probably burning in hell.

Barry realized that neither he nor Neisha considered that the deranged person responsible for taunting Neisha could be Jeannine Clark.

The tormenting telephone calls continued. The person on the phone disguised his or her voice and made vile threats. Sometimes, the person just held the phone and breathed deeply or laughed hysterically.

Neisha wondered why someone wanted to make her life so miserable!

As she sat in her office, Neisha recalled another miserable period in her life. She was in a relationship with a psychopath named Eli. If he were alive, he would be suspect number one.

Neisha met Eli at a 12-step meeting for recovering addicts. Since Eli had a significant amount of sobriety, or so he claimed, she began to date him.

At the beginning of the relationship, Eli was a perfect gentleman. He treated her like a lady. He opened doors for her and complimented her on a regular basis. He helped her financially. They considered marriage.

As time prevailed, Neisha realized if there was such a thing as a man-eater, Eli was a woman devourer. He was toxic, borderline insane. He replaced his gentlemanly attributes with verbal and emotional abuse. He called her derogatory names. The emotional abuse increased to physical abuse. He began to push her around and slap her.

On one occasion, Eli attempted to hit Neisha while she was cooking. She threw the pot of scalding hot water at him. Fortunately, he ducked and the water missed him.

Neisha told Eli that it was over.

Eli threatened to call Neisha's parole officer.

"Neisha, don't even think about breaking up with me. If you try, you will go back to prison. I'll plant drugs on you or hurt myself and tell your parole officer that you did it. You will go back to prison."

She was astonished.

"Eli, would you go through all that to be with someone who does not want to be with you?"

"Yes. Neisha, it's not over until I say it is over."

Neisha prayed to God for a way of escape.

One day, Neisha discussed the situation with Barry.

"I am so fed up with Eli and his abuse. I can't take it any longer."

"Ne, I'll talk to him. I never liked him anyway. Usually, a man who hits a woman is a coward and will not face up to another man."

Barry's powers of persuasion convinced Eli to leave Neisha alone. With Barry present, Eli retrieved his belongings from her place. That was the last time she saw him alive.

After her relationship with Eli ended, Neisha vowed to remain celibate until God revealed a husband to her.

A few years later, Eli was murdered. A woman's son killed him after Eli broke her arm and knocked out her front teeth.

Neisha attended Eli's funeral. Less than twenty people attended. Only his mother and sister spoke kindly of him.

As Eli lay still in his casket, a woman spat on him and stated, "I'm glad you're dead, you masochistic bastard."

113

The morning after the viewing of Marie's body, Neisha awakened to the sound of Barry's voice on the telephone. She knew by the strained desperation in his voice that it was Momma Flo.

Barry stated, "Mother, we are both fine. No ma'am, I am not trying to be disrespectful. Yes ma'am, I know I am never too old or too big for you to bring me down to size. I know that the Holy Spirit never leads you wrong."

Neisha grabbed clothes from the closet, showered, and hurriedly got dressed. When she exited the bathroom, Barry remained on the telephone. She eased down the stairs to the kitchen. She was not in the mood for Momma Flo and her inquisitions.

Several minutes passed before Barry yelled from the upstairs bedroom.

"Neisha, Momma wants to speak to you."

Neisha yelled back.

"Tell her that I'm cooking breakfast."

"I did. She said that you could cook and talk at the same time. Nee, please pick up the phone."

Neisha knew that she could not avoid Momma Flo. Her mother-in-law possessed an eerie gift of discernment. If Momma Flo felt that something was out of order or disturbed her spirit, she wanted answers. Neisha could also tell by the pleading tone in Barry's voice that Momma Flo was indeed giving him agony.

Neisha picked up the cordless phone in the kitchen.

"Good morning, Momma Flo. How are you?"

"How are you, daughter? Me son be trying to tell me that you all be fine, but me know better. Me spirit tells me that trouble is lurking. The devil is busy."

Neisha attempted to sound convincing.

"We are fine, Momma Flo."

"Child, you no can lie to me. You sound like de cat dat swallowed de canary."

Neisha did not want to engage in a mental or spiritual tug-of-war with Momma Flo. Neisha let down her defense. She felt relieved to share her despair.

"Momma Flo, I am exhausted. One of my best friends was murdered. Some weirdo is threatening to harm me. I just want to get away from it all."

"Neisha, me knew something was wrong. Me felt it deep in me gut. Me spirit was troubled. Last night, me was up most of de night talking to de Lord and asking Him for de revelation. Him told me to call you and Barry. Don't worry, de good Lord has not brought you and Barry dis far to leave you. Know that me love you and me be praying for you and dat son of mine. Call me any time de day or night if you need me. Now, tell Barry to get on de phone."

Neisha yelled, "Barry, Momma Flo wants you."

Neisha was tempted to eavesdrop. Instead, she mimicked Momma Flo, "Him gone catch it now."

Neisha continued preparing Barry's favorite breakfast of homemade waffles, scrambled eggs with mild cheddar cheese, and Canadian bacon. She squeezed fresh orange juice. The aroma of food and freshly brewed coffee filled the kitchen.

She summoned Barry.

"If you are not downstairs in two minutes, I am going to start eating without you."

Barry went downstairs for breakfast donned in his most ragged flannel pajamas. He knew one of Neisha's pet peeves was to come to breakfast undressed, especially if they had plans to go out. Nevertheless, he was hungry and did not want his food to get cold. He relished the aroma of his favorite breakfast as it trickled upstairs.

He greeted, "Good morning, sweetheart."

Neisha gave him an admonishing look.

"Good morning, Barry."

Barry sat down in a chair across from Neisha. He prayed over the food.

Barry drenched his waffles in buttery maple syrup. After he swallowed a morsel, he snickered. "You know that momma accused me of 'holding de truth from she'. She also told me that I was being held personally accountable for your safety."

Barry paused as his mother's voice echoed in his ear. "Boy, you better tell me when things a foul, especially if danger lurks. Me just a prayer and a plane away."

Neisha continued eating.

After a few more bites of waffles, Barry broke out laughing. When he regained his composure, he turned his attention to Neisha.

"Momma broke you down again, didn't she? I knew you would give up the goods and tell everything."

Neisha laughed as well.

"Yeah, I gave up the goods, as you so aptly put it. However, I heard the strained politeness in your voice when she felt that you were withholding information. If you had been nearby, she would have smacked you. Now, eat your breakfast before it gets cold. We must leave soon. You still have to get dressed."

After Barry got dressed, he walked downstairs to help Neisha in the kitchen.

A loud banging knock resonated on the solid oak front door of their home. The knock was simultaneous with constant ringing on the doorbell.

Barry detoured to the front door. On the other side of the peephole, trying to look inconspicuous and determine if anyone was home, stood a White man approximately five feet, eleven inches tall and 190 pounds. He sported the classic black rimmed, G-man looking sunglasses that undercover cops often wore. His hair and moustache were reddish brown. Sprinkles of red freckles covered the bridge of his nose.

Barry sized the man up as a police officer. He had enough experience dealing with law enforcement to recognize a police officer in uniform, plainclothes, or otherwise. Since he and Neisha were on the right side of the law, Barry surmised that the purpose of the man's visit was associated with Marie's murder.

As Neisha stood at the sink drying dishes, she stared out of the window at the grassy terrain in the backyard. She daydreamed about how nice it would be to have a swing set and other toys in the yard for a child. Neisha desperately wanted children.

Barry walked quietly into the kitchen. He whispered, "Hey Ne, it's Five-O at the door."

The barely audible sound of Barry's voice reached her ears. She mumbled under her breath, "That man just deflated my daydream."

"Neisha, did you hear what I just said?"

118

Irritated, she responded, "Barry, quit playing and answer the door."

"Neisha, I am serious. Come with me."

Neisha removed her apron and hung it over a chair. She folded the beige and white checkered dish towel and placed it on the rack near the stove.

Barry and Neisha walked to the front door. He opened the door slightly.

The man flashed a badge. He removed a black leather billfold from his pocket. He handed business cards to Barry and Neisha.

"Hello, Mr. and Mrs. Garrett. I am Detective John Roan from the Los Angeles Police Department, Ladera Heights Division. May I please come in?"

Barry looked puzzled.

"Are you sure that you have the right Garretts, Barry and Neisha?"

Detective Roan nodded.

Neisha asked, "Does this have something to do with Marie's murder?"

The detective shook his head.

"No ma'am. If you don't mind, I would rather come inside and discuss the purpose of my visit."

Barry replied, "Excuse our manners. Please come in. We have nothing to hide."

Barry motioned for the detective to sit on the loveseat in the living room.

Barry and Neisha sat next to each other on the matching sofa.

Neisha asked, "Detective, would you like coffee, water, or something cold to drink?"

He politely declined. "No, thank you, ma'am."

119

Detective Roan paused for several seconds.

"Mrs. Garrett, are you acquainted with Jeannine Clark?"

Neisha answered, "Yes."

"Mrs. Garrett, do you know why she would want to harm you?"

Neisha replied, "Jeannine has issues. She is in a mental institution. Why do you ask?"

Detective Roan responded, "Jeannine told her psychiatrist that she planned to kill you and bury your body where no one would find you. Shortly after, she escaped from the institution. Her whereabouts are currently unknown. The psychiatrist did not immediately contact law enforcement, although it was his ethical and legal duty to warn a potential victim or the police of such threats. We recently became aware of her threats and escape."

Neisha sat there staring at the detective with her mouth gaped wide open. She was speechless.

Barry spoke up. "Detective Roan, this is ironic. Over the past few months, my wife has received several harassing phone calls. It cannot be a coincidence. Do you have any clue concerning Jeannine's whereabouts?"

"No, Mr. Garrett. I assure you that we are trying to locate her. She attacked one of the workers at the hospital, and he sustained several serious injuries. I am not here to scare you, although you never know about people who make these types of threats. Please contact me if you hear anything. Thank you for your time. I'll be in touch."

The detective stood up.

Barry escorted Detective Roan to the door.

Neisha stood near the fireplace. She had one hand on her hip, the other on the mantle. To say that she was distraught was an understatement.

"I can't take all this. First, it was Marie's death. Now, Jeannine is on the loose."

Barry beckoned Neisha to join him on the sofa.

Neisha sat next to Barry. Her head ached. She massaged her temples with her fingers.

"Yeah, Ne. It just goes to show you that no matter how much you try to do good, evil is always present."

"Barry, that woman is insane! The only thing I ever tried to do was be her friend. How could anyone raised in the church be so demented?"

It was a rhetorical question. She knew the answer. Simply because someone went to church every Sunday, sang in the choir, or worked on the usher board did not mean that he or she had a relationship with God. Overall, the church was a sick hospital.

"Neisha, I know one thing. The police better find her crazy ass before I do. I can tap into resources that they could never dream of using."

"Barry, let the police do their job. Do not even think about contacting Carlos or any of those thugs from the past. You are a man of God. Let God take care of it."

"Well, Ne, I guess it is a good time to tell you what happened yesterday. I thought I saw Jeannine at the funeral home. The woman appeared much thinner. Somehow, in my gut, I knew it was her. I ran to the parking lot to catch up with her. She sped towards me with her car."

Neisha was livid. Her voice rose a couple of octaves.

"Are you telling me that you thought you saw Jeannine and she tried to hit you with a car?"

"Yes. I did not mention it because you were already upset."

"Barry, I was upset, but I deserved to know what was happening."

Barry felt betrayed.

"Neisha, I felt that the most important thing was for you to get through the day without having a nervous breakdown."

"Barry, I apologize. I know you had our best interests in mind."

Barry did not respond. He snatched his hand from Neisha's grip and folded his arms firmly across his chest. Silence filled the room for almost five minutes.

Barry stood up.

With a succinct tone of sarcasm in his voice, he stated, "Whenever there is excess drama in our lives, it is usually centered on your friends or your so-called sistahs. How dare you have that attitude with me? You have some nerve. I will not apologize for my actions. I would do the same thing again. I am not going anywhere."

Angry, he stormed up the stairs.

Neisha remained seated. She meditated on his comments. There had been drama on his side of the fence. Gina, the mother of his oldest daughter Letrice, freaked out when she heard Barry was getting married. They had not been together for years. Gina refused to allow him to see Letrice. She sued him for additional child support. Yet, that drama was no comparison to what Barry had experienced lately with Marie's murder, Ron's suicide, and the anonymous threats and harassment.

Neisha phoned Bettye. After several rings, it went straight to voicemail. Neisha telephoned Bettye's motel room.

Bettye answered cautiously, "Hello."

Neisha greeted, "Good morning, sis. How's everything?"

"Hey Neisha, everything's good. David arrived in town earlier than expected. He surprised me when I came to the room last night. That's why you didn't hear from me."

"Um, Bettye, that's nice. David is so thoughtful, and he loves you so much."

Bettye had an uncanny knack for reading Neisha. She denoted a sense of sadness.

"Ne, is paradise troubled?"

"Bettye, you would not believe how troubled. I need you and Dae to go to the funeral home, check on things, and greet people. Make sure that Marie's wig is glued down and that those horrible scars are covered. I am afraid that if I do not spend some time with my husband, there may not be a paradise."

"Okay, Ne, no problem. I will take the opportunity to show off my handsome husband. You know that I've got your back. I understand that husbands, home, and family come first. You must have really pissed Barry off."

"Bettye, he is upset, to say the least."

Betty asked, "Why?"

Neisha answered. "A detective just left. Jeannine is on the loose. She left a mental institution after threatening to kill me. Barry said that he thought he saw her yesterday at the funeral home. When he went outside to check, the woman tried to run him down with her car. I got an attitude because he did not tell me."

"Dang, Neisha. What the hell? Everyone knows that Jeannine is crazy for real."

"Yeah, I know. What else can happen? Anyway, thanks for covering for me. Tell David that I said hello."

"Ne, if there is anything else that I can do, call me on my cell and leave a voice message. I do not want to be bothered with Janice. She has been blowing up my phone with crazy messages."

"Okay, Bettye. I'll talk to you soon."

Bettye hung up. She lifted her hands toward heaven and prayed for Neisha and Barry.

It was rare that Barry felt disappointed in his wife. When she screwed up, she did it in a big way. He felt insulted. How dare she question him or have an attitude when his main objective was attending to their well-being!

Neisha entered the bedroom,

Barry did not acknowledge her presence. He remained seated on the lower edge of the bed. He stared at the plush chestnut brown carpet.

Neisha tried to initiate a conversation. "Barry, I spoke to Bettye. She and Dae will go to the funeral home. I am staying home."

Barry did not respond. Instead, he removed his tie and shirt. He kicked off his shoes. Barry propped a pillow against the headboard of the California King Bed, lay on the comforter, and stretched out. He turned the remote to the sports station.

Neisha leaned down and kissed his forehead.

She whispered, "Barry, I love you."

He remained aloft.

Neisha kissed his forehead again, followed by kisses on the tip of his nose, earlobes, and neck. She slowly kissed his chest and navel.

He moaned and called her name, "Neisha."

They made passionate love. For the rest of the day, they remained in solitude and enjoyed each other's company. They did not answer the phones or turn on their computers. They ministered to each other spiritually, emotionally, and physically. They could not recall the last time they spent real quality time with each other, but they agreed that it had been too long.

The morning after Detective Roan's visit, Neisha telephoned Jeannine's daughter, Vanessa.

After Jeannine abandoned Vanessa, Neisha became a surrogate mother to her. Vanessa's intense sense of obligation to Neisha was the equivalent of her hatred towards Jeannine. If she knew anything about Jeannine's whereabouts, she would not hesitate to tell it.

Vanessa answered, "Hello."

Neisha greeted, "Vanessa, how are you?"

"Auntie Ne, I am fine. How have you been? It seems like forever since we have talked."

"Vanessa, what good would it do to complain? As you know, the door and the phone are always open to you. You could call or come by. I have been extremely busy at work. Now, I am dealing with the aftermath of Marie's death."

"Auntie Ne, I am sorry about Marie. I can't believe she is gone."

Neisha responded, "Yes, I will miss her a lot. I called to ask you if Jeannine has contacted you."

Vanessa stated, "She called me several weeks ago. She tried to interrogate me about you and Uncle Barry. I told her to call you directly. She got angry, called me an ungrateful bitch, and hung up. I am glad she is in that asylum."

Neisha paused for a few seconds. "Vanessa, a detective came to warn me that Jeannine escaped, and she is out to get me."

"Auntie, she burned her bridges with everyone. I don't know where she is, and I don't care. I have firsthand experience with knowing what she is

126

capable of doing. She is demonic, one of the devil's imps. Please be careful."

"Calm down, Vanessa. If you hear anything, call me. Are you planning to attend Marie's funeral? You are welcome to ride with us."

"No thanks, Auntie Ne. I want to remember Marie the way that she was, robust and full of life. If I find out anything about Jeannine, I'll call you. I love you and Uncle Barry very much. The three of us need to get together soon. Again, please be careful."

"Vanessa, you be careful as well. We love you. See ya soon."

Neisha hung up.

On the day of Marie's funeral, security was tight. Outside Jackson's Funeral Home, reporters from several tabloid magazines and local news stations attempted to get newsworthy information or gossip.

Neisha, Barry, David, Bettye, and Dae entered the funeral home through the side door. They sat in the front row of the chapel, representing family. The women wore red, Marie's favorite color.

Most of the forty to fifty people who attended the funeral were Marie's friends, co-workers, and members of her church. Her aunts and uncles who lived on the east coast declined to attend. They were not a part of her life when she was alive. They were not interested in attending Marie's final rituals, especially once they realized that they were excluded from her will and would not receive anything."

The pastor of Marie's church, Reverend, Dr. Dwayne Ebenezer Hicks, refused to perform the funeral service. He deemed the circumstances surrounding Marie's death as scandalous. He told Neisha that Marie was an adulterous harlot whose soul went straight to hell. Ironically, he had been married four times. His former wives divorced him for adultery, physical and emotional abuse, and irreconcilable differences.

An ordained minister from Barry and Neisha's church officiated the service. The program included a viewing of slides that depicted Marie in happier times. Several people read poems or spoke of pleasant memories.

Neisha read the obituary.

Before she sat down, Neisha stated, "Marie was my Sistah in the Lord. Many people have detached from her demise. In their opinion, she died as more of an ain't than a saint. We all have sinned, and there is no such thing as a small or large sin. In God's eyes, sin is sin. Therefore, let God be the judge and worry about your salvation."

Bettye sang Mahalia Jackson's, "No More Trouble in the World." Her spirit-filled rendition hardly left a dry eye in the chapel.

The repast was held at Kujo's Banquet Hall. It was a celebration of life, not a tribute to death. People ate, drank, and danced.

Barry and David were huddled in a corner. Ron's widow, Roxanne, suddenly interrupted the jovial environment. She rambled about the room, talking loudly and randomly cursing at people.

Roxanne yelled as she walked towards Neisha.

"Your whorish friend is the reason that my Ronnie is dead. I hope she burns in hell. You should go to hell for being her friend."

Neisha did not say a word. She headed towards Roxanne.

David intervened. He ran to Roxanne and placed his arms around her in a consoling manner. He escorted her out of the building without further incident.

If Ron were alive, this would have been his brief summary of his relationship with Marie.

"I am so tired of people acting like Marie was a saint. I met her at an after party following one of my sold out concerts. At the time, I was married, although my divorce was pending.

The fact that I was married did not stop Marie from pursuing me with fervor. She chased after me like a she-dog in heat. At first, I ignored her. Then, I figured that since she was so adamant about wanting to get with a brother that I might as well take advantage. She often traveled, at her own expense, to be with me. She bought me drugs, jewelry, and spent a good deal of money on me.

Several wealthy musicians, agents, producers, and entertainers pursued her. Strange as it seemed, she chose to be with me. I became her bad habit. She was addicted to me.

My career de-escalated as my drug habit escalated. Often, I missed rehearsals or concerts because I was too high to perform. On several occasions, my publicist reported that I had the flu or suffered from exhaustion. Since heroin withdrawals mimic flu-like symptoms, it took an extremely long time for some folks to realize that drugs were the problem.

As the state of my assets and finances began to decline, I enrolled in a residential drug treatment program. I refused to have any contact with Marie during my treatment and recovery. I did not need drama or temptation. I successfully completed the program.

Based on my past escapades, it was difficult to resume my career as a solo artist in rhythm and blues. There were few reputable labels, producers, or agents willing to risk representing me. I burned many bridges when I thought that I was on top of the mountain. I found out that the valley was a lonely place.

Based on my deliverance and status as a born-again Christian, I obtained new celebrity as a gospel artist. I found the holiness and hypocrisy challenging. Many of the so-called, wannabe saints and saved folks were more deeply involved in sin than those whom they judged as sinners.

I met and subsequently married Roxanne, an employee of the gospel music production company. It was a marriage based on the Christian thing to do. She repeatedly told me that the Bible said, "It is better to marry than to burn."

Our honeymoon was more of a nightmare than a memorable experience. Roxanne put several limitations on our lovemaking. Nothing changed during the entire course of our marriage.

Irritable, restless, dissatisfied, and discontent, I knew that I was a hypocrite for perpetrating all the God and Higher Power stuff. I missed the ladies, limos, and liquor. Most of all, I missed the speedballs, cocaine mixed with heroin. The last speedball that I shot up before going to a program almost killed me, but I had one hell of a high.

Mentally, spiritually, and physically, I was in relapse mode. I stopped attending meetings. I disconnected from anything or anyone associated with trying to remain drug and alcohol free. I needed a fix, something, or someone to make me feel good.

Suddenly, and unexpectedly, Marie called. I was elated. It was as though the devil wrote a prescription for my misery.

"Hello, Ron. I was watching a cable Christian Network a few months ago when lo and behold, I saw you. I am so glad that you are saved and delivered. I recommitted myself to Christ as well."

"Marie, ooh, how good to hear your voice. I was thinking about you just the other day. Perhaps, we can get together."

"Sure Ron. Give me a call."

"Marie, hold the line while I grab a pen so I can write down those digits."

I convinced Marie to have lunch with me. After a few months, I coerced her into sleeping with me. I left Roxanne and moved in with Marie. The devil put out the bait, and Marie and I bit the entire hook, line, and sinker. We were two consenting adults.

Our relationship was a roller coaster ride of highs and lows. The more my life became unmanageable, the more I loathed Marie. Instead of providing some sort of sanity, a safe haven, and the stability that I needed, she started messing around with dope. She tricked out. I did us both a favor by taking us out of this stinking world."

The morning after Marie's funeral, Bettye awakened before David. She ordered room service. She checked her cell phone. Janice left several messages. Bettye was fed up.

After they ate, Bettye grabbed David's hand.

"Baby, I need to talk to you. Please do not interrupt me. Promise you will not say anything until I finish talking."

He nodded his head.

David stated, "Bettye, I don't know what you thought that your mother could accomplish by trying to blackmail you. I can't believe that you allowed her to get away with it. You know how much I love you. I knew enough about your past that it did not matter to me. I am only concerned about our future. We all have sinned and fallen short."

Bettye telephoned Neisha later that day.

"Well, Ms. Neisha, I called to invite you to lunch so that you can gloat and say, 'I told you so.' I confessed everything to David. He did not seem surprised or shocked. Soon, I'll share my testimony at church. I hope you and Barry will come to Atlanta and show your support."

Neisha laughed. "You think that you know me so well. I am not going to say I told you so. Hah! Instead, I will hum it."

Neisha hummed.

Bettye laughed. "Sometimes, I can't stand you."

"Ah, Bettye, you know you love me. Of course, Barry and I will come to Atlanta. We need a vacation."

"Thanks, my Neisha. I knew I could count on you. We can talk more about it at lunch tomorrow."

"Your treat? I'll pick an expensive place. Bettye, Janice is not going to be happy once you cut her off."

"Yeah, Ne, I know. I'll handle it. Neisha, how is Dae?"

"She is holding her own. I can tell that her soul is grieved. I'll keep praying for her."

"Me too. I love you."

"Back at ya."

Neisha hung up.

Marie named Neisha as her beneficiary. Neisha inherited Marie's home, cars, and personal belongings.

Prior to the unwanted task of going to Marie's home and taking an inventory of Marie and Ron's possessions, Neisha telephoned Roxanne.

"Hello Roxanne, it is Neisha. How are you?"

Roxanne's voice had an icy chill to it.

"Hello Neisha. I am fine. What do you want?"

Neisha replied, "I am going to the house to pack up Ron and Marie's belongings. Do you want his things sent to you?"

Roxanne began to cry. Between sobs, she stated, "Only if the items have monetary value. I cannot live on sentiment. The insurance company will not pay on Ron's policy because his death was ruled a suicide, and he was under the influence of illegal drugs. After he died, his record sales skyrocketed for a moment. I am waiting for some royalty checks. I'll probably file for bankruptcy. Ron was in debt up to his neck. He is dead, but his debts live on."

"Roxanne, if there is anything I can do to help, please let me know."

"Thanks Neisha. I guess you can have his things sent to me if it is not too much trouble."

"Fine. When I have everything packed, I'll call you. I'll be praying for you. Goodbye, Roxanne."

Neisha hung up. She wrote a check for Roxanne from her personal account for $2500.

Neisha arrived at Marie's home. Pieces of broken yellow police tape marked, "Do Not Cross, Crime Scene," remained scattered in the yard. A few pieces of the tape were pinned to the front door. Neisha angrily snatched the tape and threw it down on the porch.

Inside the home, everything appeared intact. There was no indication of looters or squatters. In the master bedroom, where the bodies were found, faint traces of orange chalk outlined the imprint of Ron's body. Blood stains highlighted the comforter where Marie was discovered on the bed.

Neisha felt nauseous. She opened the windows and closed the door to the bedroom. She also opened windows throughout the home to allow fresh air to ventilate.

As she stood in the living room, Neisha decided to start her mission by searching Marie's hall closet. She found a tiny key hidden in one of Marie's hatboxes. She used the key to unlock a small chest. Inside, she found a box of porno movies and drug paraphernalia. Neisha gasped in shock. If the items belonged to Dae, she would not be surprised. But Marie was a different story.

Neisha also found Marie's journal. A part of her felt that reading it would be an invasion of Marie's privacy. Yet, there might be some answers that would help explain the darkness that overshadowed her friend's life.

Neisha began reading. To say that she was amazed would be an understatement. The journal disclosed the resentments Marie held against her father, the incestuous relationship, and Marie's abortion.

As Neisha scanned through the journal, further details of Marie's divorces and various relationships, as well as her addiction to sex and drugs, were revealed. Marie was into sadism and masochism. She enjoyed receiving and inflicting pain. She indulged in orgies, adultery, porn, and other strongholds of darkness. In some, sadistic, twisted way, it brought her pleasure and temporary gratification.

Neisha's body shuddered. She concluded that it is amazing how you think you know someone but realize you barely knew that person at all. The person described in the journal was not the Marie that Neisha thought she knew.

An urge to close the journal and burn it struck Neisha, but her curiosity had reached a peak. She flipped through several pages at the end. In Marie's last journal entries, dated a week before the horrific murder-suicide, she wrote that she was involved with another man.

In another entry, Marie wrote, "I can't stand this life with Ron anymore. I deserve better. Ron is angry because he found out that I have been seeing another man on the side, and I am on the waiting list for a drug program. I could ask Neisha to help me get into a program. However, I, Marie Danielle Johnson, need to stand on my own two feet. Yet, I get a strange feeling that if I do not move on immediately, my life will be over. Maybe God is warning me that His grace and mercy towards me are running out."

Neisha's reading was interrupted by an unexpected knock at the door. She peeked out the window shades in the dining room. It was Marie's busy body neighbor, Mrs. Robinson.

Mrs. Robinson could often be observed hosing her lawn, standing on the porch, or peeking out the window.

Mrs. Robinson was a brown-skinned, petite woman who wore an auburn colored, shoulder-length wig. Her ill-fitted dentures often clicked when she spoke.

Neisha opened the door.

"Hello, Mrs. Robinson."

"Neisha, I came to see if I could be of assistance."

"No thanks. I am just assessing how much work needs to be done around here."

"Well, Neisha, I would like to come in and talk to you for a few moments if you don't mind. Marie probably left this house to you, and it is yours now."

Neisha knew that Mrs. Robinson was fishing for an answer regarding the status of Marie's home. She did not bite at the bait.

"Come in."

Mrs. Robinson stood in the middle of the living room.

"Neisha, I belong to the neighborhood lookout committee. I try to keep my eye on things. On the evening before Marie was murdered, I was outside watering the grass. I heard an intense argument between two men and a woman. Shortly after, I saw a man leaving the home. I did not call the police because Marie and Ron were always arguing, partying, or having some drama. I did not see Ron or Marie the next day. A couple of days passed, and I hadn't seen either of them. I went to a phone booth and called 911. The police arrived hours later. You know they take their own sweet time coming around here."

Mrs. Robinson paused to scratch at her hair.

"My head is itching. You know it does that when your hair is growing. I got a lot of hair up under this wig. It costs too much to keep it up."

Neisha smiled.

"Please continue."

"As I was saying, the door must have been open because the uniformed cops just walked in. The next thing I knew, the place was swarming with uniformed police, plain-clothed detectives, and the coroner's wagon. Then, I saw two body bags being rolled out on gurneys. I would have called you if I had your number. I know that you and Marie were tight. She always spoke highly of you."

Neisha held back tears.

"Thanks for the information, Mrs. Robinson. I will pass it on to the detectives handling the case. Here is my number. If you remember anything else or see any activity around the house, please call me. I'll walk you to the door."

"Neisha, I'm sorry for your loss. Goodbye."

Neisha shut and locked the windows. She grabbed her purse and the journal. Neisha realized that she needed to get help with cleaning out the house. She hoped no more surprises lurked in the closets.

As she drove home, Neisha's thoughts were filled with the tragic circumstances that surrounded Marie's life and death. She wondered who the man was that Mrs. Robinson heard arguing with Marie and Ron. The possibilities were endless.

Approximately a month later, Barry and Neisha sat in the pulpit of David and Bettye's church in Atlanta. The attendees represented the not-so-usual Sunday crowd. Before the service, a free meal was served. Many came to the church for a nutritional meal. Some remained for spiritual nourishment.

Barry opened the service with prayer.

Neisha led praise and worship.

Bettye delivered an auspicious message. She shared her testimony about her past. She also explained how she allowed the devil to hold her hostage with emotional extortion and captivity. She concluded that what the enemy used for evil, God turned around for her good.

The church was on fire. The anointing and power of the Holy Spirit were present. Several people began speaking in tongues. Many others fell out at the altar, slain in the Spirit. Young men approached the altar holding the waistbands of their pants, so they didn't sag. Gang members removed various colored bandanas from their heads and pockets that represented gang affiliations.

The ushers passed out brown paper bags. Bettye beseeched the congregation to deposit anything in their possession from which they needed deliverance.

People of all ages deposited shot bottles of liquor, cigarettes, condoms, and other paraphernalia in the bags.

A female member of the church approached Bettye.

"Sister Bettye, I have been holding on to this wedding ring for five years, hoping that my husband would return to me. The reality is that he has moved on. Take this ring, sell it, and donate the money to the church."

"Are you sure, Sister Liz? This is an expensive ring."

Liz confirmed, "Yes, I am sure."

Bettye hugged her. "Thanks, I will send you a receipt."

A young, White man asked to speak to Bettye and David alone. His appearance was disheveled; he looked as if he had not slept in days. His face had several tiny craters that resembled tweak marks of an addict.

"Uh, hello, pastor and first lady. I robbed an old couple, and I came inside the church to hide out until things cooled down. God must have preordained my steps to be here. I feel so convicted. Please return these items to the rightful owners."

He gave David a bag containing jewelry, cash, and a wallet. He tearfully begged him not to identify him to the police. The young man promised that he would change his life.

David asked, "Son, would you like for us to pray for you now?"

"No thanks, pastor. I will be in touch."

The young man ran out of the building.

Bettye looked puzzled.

"David, I have seen that boy before. I think he is Congressman Fairchild's son."

"You might be right."

They returned to the pulpit.

Immediately after the service, David telephoned the watch commander at the local police department. He requested that officers be dispatched to confiscate the illegal items that were collected. Officers arrived within fifteen minutes.

On their way home, David and Bettye drove to the address on the elderly couple's identification. They returned the stolen items to the couple.

The couple was ecstatic and promised to attend services the following week.

Bettye mailed a tape of the service to her conniving mother as an official seal of deliverance. She enclosed a check and a handwritten note.

"Mother use this money wisely. Your days of extortion and blackmail are over. I am no longer captive to your misery. Love, Bettye."

Barry and Neisha remained in Atlanta for a week.

On one beautiful, starry night, Barry stood on the balcony of the hotel and looked towards heaven. He prayed that God would bless him and Neisha with a child of their own. He thought he saw a falling star. He believed it was confirmation of his prayer.

When Barry went inside, Neisha lay on the bed, reading a novel. He gently removed it from her hands.

"Ne, we have to get away more often. I miss the quality time we used to share."

Neisha agreed. "Yes, I know. It seems as though we work harder at not working hard. At my last appointment, Doc Webster suggested that a getaway might be just what we needed. He still could not find any reason for my not conceiving a baby. I know it will happen in God's timing. Maybe, the time is now."

Barry turned off the tulip-shaped lamps mounted on the wall above the nightstands.

They made love.

In late November, Barry noticed several physical and emotional changes in his wife. Neisha became irritable for no reason, her moods fluctuated, and she gained several pounds. By mid-December, things worsened. Neisha complained of nausea and vomited throughout the day.

As destiny would have it, Barry arrived home from work early. Neisha's car was parked in the driveway.

Barry entered the house. He called out to Neisha. She did not answer. He heard anguishing, moaning sounds coming from their bedroom. Frantically, he zoomed up the stairs two at a time.

He found Neisha lying on the bed, her body twisted like a pretzel. She looked drained and feeble.

Barry asked, "Ne, are you okay?'

She replied, "Yeah, I think I am coming down with the flu or getting an ulcer or something."

Barry stated, "Ne, maybe you are pregnant. It might be morning sickness."

Initially, she laughed. A few seconds later, she accused Barry of being cruel. She cried.

Barry exited the room. He was midway down the staircase when he shouted, "Ne, I'll be back shortly. I'm going to the store."

Before she could object, he got in his car and drove to a nearby store to purchase a home pregnancy kit.

Barry proceeded through the checkstand and removed the items from the cart.

Evan, the cashier, began ringing up the purchases. As he noticed the pregnancy kit, he smiled, revealing light-blue colored braces on his upper and lower teeth. He had been acquainted with Neisha and Barry for some time. He inquired about the purchase. He whispered, "Mr. Barry, is Ms. Neisha pregnant?"

"Evan, I am praying that she is."

"Sir, I will be praying for you both. Y'all will make wonderful parents," remarked Evan.

"Thank you, Evan."

Barry paid for the items.

In the parking lot, a woman in a wheelchair panhandled money for food. Her right leg was amputated below the knee. She was neatly groomed.

Barry removed $10 from his wallet and gave it to her.

She exclaimed, "Thank you, mister. I'm starving!"

Barry stated, "You are welcome. What is happening with you?"

She pointed towards her leg.

"Diabetes, I had to have it amputated. Every month, I give my brother money for rent and food. He squanders the money. I want to move, but it is difficult being handicapped and on a fixed income. I tried a few shelters, but that life was not for me. I would rather work. I have skills."

Barry gave her one of Neisha's business cards.

"Call my wife. She may be able to help you. Tell her that I referred you."

"Thanks again. Tell your wife that Nell will call her."

She swiftly wheeled her chair inside the store.

When Barry returned home, Neisha remained in the same fetal position on the bed. He removed the pregnancy kit from the bag and handed it to her.

"Neisha, go to the bathroom and read the directions. No arguments."

Lethargically, she rose slowly from the bed and went into the bathroom.

Minutes later, a loud shrieking sound came from the bathroom. Barry rushed in. He found Neisha standing near the sink, trembling and crying.

Neisha held the device in her hand. The indicator read "positive."

"Barry, according to this test, I may be pregnant."

He shouted, "Thank God for answering prayers. Hallelujah."

"Barry, before we get too excited, I am going to Doc Webster's office the first thing in the morning. Sometimes, these tests do not provide accurate results."

"Okay, Ne. The sooner that we know, the sooner we can start making plans."

Neisha tossed and turned in bed throughout the night. She talked about baby names and decorating a nursery until she finally dozed off.

The following morning, Neisha woke up at the crack of dawn. She telephoned Yavette and informed her that she was taking the day off. Then, she telephoned the doctor's office.

"Good Morning, Webster's Medical Group. This is Sara speaking. How may I help you?"

"Good morning, Sara, how are you? It is Neisha Garrett. I must see Doc Webster today, preferably this morning. I took a home pregnancy test last night. The results were positive. Please squeeze me in. I need confirmation, one way or the other."

Sara paused. She knew that Barry and Neisha had been trying to have a baby. She was more than willing to make an accommodation. Sara also knew that if Dr. Webster found out she denied Neisha an appointment, he would have a hissy fit.

"Neisha, I can squeeze you in at 11:00."

Neisha responded, "Fine, I will see you then. Thank you so much. God bless you."

Neisha hung up.

At approximately 10:15 am, Neisha arrived at Dr. Webster's office. Shortly after her arrival, the medical assistant, Katrina, took Neisha's vitals.

Katrina used a butterfly needle to withdraw several vials of Neisha's blood. She obtained a urine sample and sent the specimens to the lab for processing. She labeled the envelope – RUSH-STAT.

"Ms. Neisha, your lab test results will return shortly. Your blood pressure is a little low, but there is no reason to be alarmed. You've gained seven pounds since your last visit two months ago."

Neisha complained. "Over the past several weeks, I have had an appetite like a horse. I have had periods of feeling extremely fatigued and cold. I think I may be a bit anemic."

Katrina stated, "We should know more soon. Please wait in the lobby until I call you."

After what seemed like an eternity, Katrina summoned Neisha to follow her to *Exam Room 5*. She handed Neisha the standard blue medical gown.

"Ms. Neisha, please remove everything. Leave the gown open in the back. Dr. Webster will be with you shortly."

"Thanks, Katrina."

Doctor Paul Webster is a sixty-something year old African American obstetrician-gynecologist. He is approximately five feet, ten inches tall with a small, wiry frame. His gold-plated metal glasses rest snugly on the bridge of his nose. The crown of his head is bald. The lower back of his head resembles the shape of a crescent moon trimmed with salt and pepper hair.

He prefers to be addressed as Doc Webster. He established his practice over 30 years ago in inner city Los Angeles. He has two offices and hires people from the community. In his free time, he provides free medical services to uninsured parolees. His wife died several years ago. He deplores being a widower.

Doc Webster sat in his office and reviewed Neisha Garrett's test results. In the past, he had the unfortunate task of advising Neisha that he could not provide a scientific explanation why she had not gotten pregnant. He remembered that she always responded with hope and faith. "Doc, a miracle can override a medical mystery. I will get pregnant in God's timing if God so desires. If not, Barry and I will consider adoption."

Approximately fifteen minutes after Neisha sat impatiently in *Exam Room 5*, Doc Webster knocked on the door. He entered the room, accompanied by a nurse.

Doc Webster acted clueless.

"Neisha, what brings you here today?"

Neisha replied, "A positive home pregnancy test."

Doc Webster smiled. He directed Neisha to put her feet in the metal, cold stirrups.

"Neisha, everything seems fine. I estimate that you and Barry will become parents in mid to late August."

Tears of joy streamed down Neisha's face. She opened her mouth, but words did not come forth.

While Neisha was speechless, Doc Webster seized the opportunity to discuss prenatal care.

"Neisha, you have suffered a couple of miscarriages. Do take care of yourself. Hire extra help, if necessary. Monitor your stress. For God's sake, learn to relax. I will call in your prescriptions for iron and prenatal vitamins. Sara will make your return appointment."

Neisha replied, "Doc, I am so excited. I will be mindful of all your instructions."

"You can start by getting dressed and calling your husband to share the good news.

Doc Webster and the nurse exited the room.

Neisha got dressed quickly. She stopped at the desk to make her return appointment before entering the lobby.

Barry stood in a corner. In one hand, he held a dozen roses. In the other, he held a box of Neisha's favorite chocolate-covered pecan candy.

Neisha asked. "Barry, what are you doing here?"

"Ne, did you think I would let you do this without me?"

She smiled.

"The baby is due in August."

Barry yelled, "Thank you, Jesus."

He gave Neisha her gifts and kissed her on the lips.

Sara and Katrina peeked through the reception window. Katrina gave the couple a thumbs-up sign of approval.

B arry and Neisha celebrated their good news by dining at the "Skipper's Table".

Heather was no longer employed there. She owned a successful business as a caterer and wedding planner. Sean actually did become an Emmy-nominated actor. He starred as a gay cop in a weekly, nighttime drama.

Barry practically monopolized the conversation during lunch.

"Neisha, now that you are pregnant, you will no longer work 10-12 hours a day. You will watch your diet and quit eating all that junk and fast food. Now that father-to-be Garrett has spoken, what instructions did Dr. Webster give you?'

Neisha answered, "He wants me to take it easy, slow down, take prenatal vitamins, you know."

Barry agreed.

"My sentiments exactly. Ne, you need to hire additional full-time help at work."

"I will soon, I promise."

"Not soon, Neisha, but immediately!"

She knew he was serious.

"Okay. I'll start working on it next week."

The happy couple telephoned Momma Flo that evening.

"Hello, praises to God," Momma Flo greeted.

Barry asked, "Hi, mom, how are you?"

Momma Flo stated, "Well, me be feeling fine for an old lady. How be my favorite son and daughter-in-law?

Barry laughed.

"I'm your only son. Anyway, we are both fine. We have news for you."

"What news ?" asked Momma Flo.

Barry teased, "Only son seems to be forgetful."

"Boy, you quit playing."

"Mom, you have no sense of humor. Anyway, you are going to be a grandmother again."

Mother Flo bombarded him with questions,

"When did you find out? When de baby due? Is Neisha taking vitamins and eating right?"

Barry attempted to answer.

Momma Flo interrupted, "Let me talk to Neisha. Me never get de full truth from you."

Neisha laughed.

"Momma Flo, please calm down. We have the speaker on. I hear you loud and clear. I am fine. Last night, I received a positive result from a home pregnancy test. I received confirmation from Dr. Webster today. Of course, you are the first person we told. The baby is due sometime in August."

Momma Flo sounded only slightly convinced.

"Umm. Of course. Me been waiting for dis news. Well, dis is de confirmation. Me got news

156

too. De good Lord has told me to leave Louisiana. Deidre also wants to spend more time wid Barry. We be moving to Los Angeles. Now is good time. We help with de baby."

Neisha and Barry stared at each other. Shocked, they did not know how to respond.

Momma Flo gave them a moment to digest what she said.

"We can talk later, though me mind pretty made up. The good Lord has spoken. When Him speaks, me listen."

Barry stated, "Fine, momma. Of course, whatever you decide is fine with us. We are here for you. Neisha and I have a lot to discuss. We will call you in a few days. We love you."

"Me love you both. Bye."

Momma Flo hung up.

Barry set the receiver on the base of the phone. He glared at the wall.

Neisha, knowing her husband all too well, inquired, "Okay, honey, what are you thinking?"

"I am worried about mom. She wants to leave Louisiana. She has lived there all her life. Do you think she is ill? Is there something that she is not telling us?"

Neisha attempted to reassure him.

"No baby. Momma Flo is fine. You know how she is. She says the Lord told her to move. For her, that settles it. She probably thinks my pregnancy is the confirmation that she needed. It is a good thing."

The look on Barry's face indicated that he was still skeptical.

Neisha changed the subject. "I am so excited. We are finally going to have a baby."

"Ne, we have tons of things to discuss and plan. This will be no picnic in the park given your past miscarriages."

"Barry, you worry too much. For now, I want to relish the fact that we are going to be parents. There is not a lot to plan. We have resources and room. Bettye and David will be the child's godparents. If anything happened to us, Momma Flo would not relinquish custody of her grandchild to anyone. Therefore, Momma Flo will be the guardian. I will continue working and hire extra help. If the baby is a girl, we will name her Jenna Flomarie Garrett after Ms. Jenna, Momma Flo, and Marie." If the baby is a boy, he'll be named Barry Lamont Garrett II after his knucklehead daddy."

Barry laughed. "So, you think that you have it all figured out."

Neisha confirmed. "I do."

"Well, then whatever you say is fine with me, wifey."

Neisha sat on his lap and began to undress.

"For now, hubby, let's reenact how babies are made."

He removed her clothing.

That evening, Barry and Neisha telephoned David and Bettye to ask if they would be their baby's godparents.

Bettye and David were extremely excited for them. They did not hesitate to say yes.

Neisha and Betty talked for nearly an hour before Barry reminded her that they needed to eat dinner.

"Ne, I am sure that Betty and David have eaten. It is three hours ahead in Atlanta."

Neisha placed her hand over the phone. "Ok. Let me say goodbye to Bettye."

During dinner, the upcoming birth of their baby remained the topical conversation piece.

It appeared that the dark clouds over their lives had subsided. Things were looking brighter. They were happy. Neisha had not received a threatening telephone call in over one week.

"Barry, I want to do everything the old-fashioned way. I do not want to know the sex of our child before he or she is born. I will deliver the baby naturally, no drugs. We will attend Lamaze classes. You will be my coach."

He nodded. But Barry sat there thinking of how to expedite efforts to find insane Jeannine.

Jeannine Clark grew up in a middle-class family. She had two younger brothers and one younger sister. The family migrated to California when she was 10 years old.

Jeannine's father, Thaddeus, was self-employed as a carpenter. Jeannine genuinely loved her father.

Margaret, Jeannine's mother, was a seamstress. She designed clothing and hats, mostly church attire. Jeannine described her mother as old-fashioned, overprotective, and overbearing. She despised her mother.

Margaret was born and raised in a holiness church. Although it has been said that people who are saved and filled with the Holy Ghost do not fear witchcraft, superstition, and the unknown associated with the so-called supernatural, Margaret was exceptionally superstitious.

During lightning and thunderstorms, Margaret forced the children to cover all the mirrors and windows in the house with sheets or blankets, unplug all electrical items, and take the phone off the hook.

Margaret's other superstitious idiosyncrasies that she imposed on the children were that they dared not walk under ladders, split poles, break a mirror, or allow a black cat to cross their paths. Neighbors thought that her family was a bit strange.

Margaret often accused Thaddeus of cheating with other women. She would withhold sex and anything else from him that she thought caused him to suffer. She checked his pants for phone numbers, his shirt collars for lipstick stains, and his underwear.

Thaddeus, a firm believer in his marital vows, was dedicated to Margaret. The stress and accusations became overwhelming. He filed for divorce.

Jeannine had a beautiful face and features. She resembled a porcelain doll. However, she was obese, short, and squat. Whenever she was depressed, which was more often than not, she ate. Yet, it was not her outward appearance that turned people off, but her sullen and pessimistic personality. She dispelled the myth that fat people were jolly. She kept creating chaos and drama wherever she went. She was always in somebody's business. She was addicted to gossip. Her personal life was a mess.

Good-looking men were her source of validation. She tried to obtain envy from other women by being on the arm of a handsome man. On the contrary, most women did not envy Jeannine but wondered how much she paid to be with those men.

Jeannine was unwed when she became pregnant. She refused to disclose any information regarding the father to her parents.

Margaret abhorred the thought of having an illegitimate grandchild. She concocted a story that Jeannine's husband was in the military. She informed Jeannine that as long as she lived under her roof, she would go along with it. Jeannine even wore a wedding ring and relocated to another state to live with relatives until the baby was born. Jeannine gave birth to a beautiful baby girl, Vanessa.

Although she hated school, she sought a career as a nurse.

As a registered nurse, Jeannine earned good money. She squandered most of her earnings on men and trying to keep up with the Joneses. Vanessa attended private school. Jeannine leased cars because her credit was bad. Despite all the external stimuli such as cars, clothes, and other tangible things, Jeannine remained unfulfilled, sullen, and unsatisfied.

Since Jeannine worked with terminally ill and hospice clients, she often helped herself to extra money, narcotic medication, and pieces of jewelry. She had no remorse in taking advantage of anyone, including the ill and elderly. Yet, she was in church every Sunday, trying to showboat in designer clothes and jewelry. She sat at the far side with the celebrities and the wannabes.

Jeannine and Kenneth met in a parking lot at the mall. Kenneth was well-dressed and carried several bags. He offered to help Jeannine, the consummate shopper, put her purchases in the trunk of her car. Little did she know that Kenneth frequented the mall to meet women or shoplift from stores.

After Jeannine drove away, he proceeded to the bus stop.

They began dating. Kenneth made up excuses why he could not pick up Jeannine in a car or why she could not visit his apartment. The truth was that Kenneth lived with his baby's mama, and he did not have a car.

Kenneth moved in with Jeannine. He was arrested and sentenced to prison for shoplifting and possession of drugs.

They exchanged marital vows while he was in prison. Jeannine was ecstatic. They consummated their marriage in the prison motel where rooms were set aside for married couples. She visited him regularly.

After Kenneth was released, he moved in with Jeannine. The first few months of marital life were good. Soon, he tired of Jeannine's controlling, jealous, and erratic behavior. She constantly reminded him that she was in control, and that he lived in her apartment, drove her car, and ate her food.

One day, while Jeannine was at work, Kenneth packed his things and moved back in with his baby's mama.

As payback, Jeannine contacted Kenneth's parole officer and accused him of molesting Vanessa. He received a parole violation and a new charge of sexual misconduct with a minor. He was sentenced to five years.

Despite her responsibility for his incarceration, Jeannine sent him letters, money, and packages.

As a condition of Kenneth's parole, he was mandated to register as a sex offender. He soon realized that having a criminal record was a barrier in itself, but the additional label of sex offender made it worse.

Kenneth's search for housing led him to the crime-ridden areas of McArthur Park and downtown Skid Row. He could not stand living among derelicts. His baby's mother had gotten married. He could not return to live with her.

The only work he found was doing day labor or construction. Feeling defeated, he reunited with Jeannine despite all that had taken place. After all, they were still married.

An additional stipulation of Kenneth's parole condition was that he could not live in the same residence as Vanessa. Jeannine sent Vanessa to live with an uncle. She chose her man over her daughter.

When a better opportunity arose with an older, financially secure woman, Kenneth abandoned Jeannine again.

Jeannine demanded that Vanessa return home. She resumed her role as mother to Vanessa as if nothing ever happened.

Miserable and emotionally distraught, Jeannine sat alone in her room, thinking about the sad turn of events. When she escaped from the hospital, Jeannine did not intend to hurt anyone. She lost control when they attempted to stop her.

For the life of her, she could not understand why she had grown to despise Neisha so much. It seemed that after Neisha became saved and sober, they had very little in common. Neisha would not hang out with her at the malls or nightclubs. The more God blessed Neisha, the more Jeannine despised her. She became obsessed with making Neisha's life miserable.

Jeannine recalled that she and Neisha met at a nightclub. Neisha was hanging out with several of her girlfriends, dancing, drinking, and having a good time. Neisha approached the booth where Jeanine sat.

"Hello, my name is Neisha. I need to sit down before I fall. Do you mind if I sit in your booth for a while?"

Jeannine shook her head.

"Hi, I am Jeannine. Have a seat."

Neisha flopped down.

"Jeannine, would you like a drink?"

"Oh no, Neisha, I don't drink alcohol, do drugs, or anything like that. I am saved and filled with the Holy Ghost."

Neisha lifted her hand for the waitress.

The waitress zigzagged her way through the crowded dance floor to the booth. Neisha ordered a

Long Island Iced Tea for herself and a Virgin Margarita for Jeannine.

Neisha looked at Jeannine through her slightly bloodshot eyes.

"Jeannine, I don't mean to offend you, but if you are so saved and all that, what are you doing here at this club on a Saturday night? Oh, never mind, don't answer that. There are probably plenty of saved folks in here. They will get their booty call on tonight and be praising the Lord tomorrow. Screw all that saved and church stuff."

Jeannine did not respond.

"Well, Jeannine, let me ask you another question. Why are you sitting here looking miserable?"

"Neisha, no one has asked me to dance. My friends are all socializing and having a good time. I am holding down the booth."

"Jeannine, I don't let that stop me. I ask someone to dance with me, or I dance by myself. Then again, I have a lot of courage when I am drinking. The more I drink, the more courage I get."

Jeannine laughed.

A fairly attractive man asked Jeannine to dance.

Jeannine hesitated.

Neisha encouraged her. "Girl, go dance. I got the booth."

Jeannine sashayed her wide hips out to the dance floor. She danced to a couple of fast jams. When a slow record came on, she returned to the booth. She had a huge grin on her face, looking like a Cheshire Cat.

"Whew! Neisha, he asked for my number. I gave it to him, but I probably won't talk to him. He works for the city sanitation department on a trash truck. That means he goes home smelling like garbage. Ugh."

Neisha threw her head back and laughed.

"Girl, at least he is a BMW."

Jeannine looked puzzled. She asked, "What is a "BMW?"

Neisha laughed again.

"Girl, a Black Man Working. Better yet, he got benefits. No one said that you had to marry him or sleep with him. Talk to him and see what he is about. Now, I see why you were sitting here alone. Men can read that stuck-up attitude."

Jeannine and Neisha finished their drinks.

At approximately the same time, the DJ's voice resonated through the speakers.

"It is the last call for alcohol. You've got another 20 minutes before we shut it down. I don't know where you are going, but you gotta get outta here. Free condoms are available by the exit doors."

Ultimately, Jeannine and Neisha began to hang out together. They went to malls, clubs, dances, and other social outings. Neisha would not accompany her to church. She usually had a hangover from the night before.

Over time, Neisha distanced herself. Jeannine felt abandoned and rejected. Jeannine did not deal well with rejection.

A few weeks after Doc Webster confirmed her pregnancy, Neisha felt particularly joyful. She was dusting the mantle over the fireplace when the telephone rang. She gleefully answered, "Praise the Lord."

On the other end of the phone was Jeannine. It was as if the devil took a reprieve from hell and finally made her presence known. She was her usual sarcastic and unpleasant self.

"You definitely should praise the Lord since it seems He continues to bless you. I still don't know how I have been saved all my life, yet you continue to receive blessings while I continue to go through hell."

Neisha exchanged the sarcasm.

"Hell to the o, Jeannine, how are you? It is good to hear from you. Well, at least I have been waiting for you to stop breathing heavy, disguising your voice, and playing on the phone. I hope that all is well with you. So, I heard that you escaped from the insane asylum and threatened to kill me. Aside from that, what else is new?"

With the cordless phone in hand, Neisha walked into the den where Barry studied his message. She placed her hand over the phone and whispered, "Barry, it is Jeannine."

He immediately stopped what he was doing.

Neisha put the phone on speaker. She waited for Jeannine's response. After all, there must have been a method to Jeannine's madness, a reason for her call.

"Neisha, you turned my daughter and husband against me. Now, you have the nerve to be pregnant, married, and have a few zeros in your bank account. You ruined my life, you make me sick, and you must suffer."

Neisha yawned.

"Yada, yada, yada, Jeannine. You sound like the same old broken record. I am not responsible for turning Vanessa or anyone else against you. What did you expect? You tried to kill your daughter and had your husband falsely incarcerated. You ruined my credit and stole from me. You can take full responsibility for the fact that no one wants you involved in their lives."

The tone and volume of Jeannine's voice increased to a shrill reminiscent of the annoying sound of chalk screeching on a blackboard.

"Neisha, don't try to be all sanctified with me. Look outside your front door. It is going to take Jesus and a band of angels to protect you from me."

Neisha's chest heaved up and down as her breath shortened.

"Jeannine, you are crazy as hell. You really need to take your medication. I have never done anything to you but tried to be your friend. After I realized that you meant me more harm than good, I left you alone. You do not pump fear into my heart. You are a coward. That is why you do sneaky, underhanded things. I dare you to face me woman to woman. If you think that Jesus has to call a regiment of angels for you, then you have life twisted. Anyway, the last laugh on the devil belongs to God. Goodbye."

Neisha slammed the phone on the desk and headed for the front door.

Barry grabbed her arm.

"Neisha, you have no idea what that utterly disturbed woman may have put on the front porch or when she put it there. We have not been outside since we arrived home last night. Calm down. You are not going out there and neither am I. Just hold on for a few moments while I figure out what to do."

Neisha nodded. She paced back and forth.

Barry telephoned Detective Roan.

Surprisingly, the detective answered.

Barry outlined the details of the phone call from Jeannine.

"Detective, can you help us?"

"Mr. Garrett, it just so happens that I am at the station catching up on some paperwork. I will grab a couple of officers. We should be there within twenty minutes. Do not go outside."

Barry and Neisha waited in the living room for Detective Roan's arrival.

A distraught Neisha rocked back and forth on the sofa. She repeated emphatically, "The battle is not mine; it is the Lord's. No weapon formed against me will prosper."

"Neisha, please calm down for your sake and the baby's. Jeannine planned to upset you, and she did that".

"Barry, do you know how bad I want to lay some real hands on that woman?"

"Yes, I know. I am fighting with my own demons when it comes to dealing with Jeannine. "

Detective Roan arrived at the Garrett home in an unmarked police car. Shortly thereafter, two uniformed officers arrived in a black and white squad car.

As the trio walked towards the door, Detective Roan called Barry from his cell phone.

"Hello," Barry answered.

"Mr. Garrett, we are here. Please remain inside until I am sure that it is safe."

A brown shoebox, with a lid, was positioned approximately five feet from the front door. Detective Roan approached it cautiously and listened carefully for noise. Feeling confident that there was no ticking sound, he extended the narrow end of a billy club and tipped the lid from the box.

The uniformed officers watched as Detective Roan removed an African artifact of a pregnant woman. A knife protruded from a hole carved in the mid-section of the stomach. A rope, in the form of a noose, hung around the neck of the statuette.

Convinced that it was a message from a possible psychopath, but posed no immediate threat, Detective Roan dismissed the officers.

The detective rang the doorbell.

Barry answered the door and invited the detective in.

Detective Roan sat down on the love seat. He displayed the contents of the box to Barry and Neisha.

"I will have everything dusted for prints. I doubt that there will be any."

Neisha's agitation surfaced.

Neisha shrieked, "You don't need any prints to know who is responsible for this. It was Jeannine's insane ass! What are you doing to find her?"

"Ms. Garrett, we are doing what we can to locate her. Since this incident occurred, we should be able to increase our efforts."

Neisha did not respond. She was not convinced. Increased efforts did not mean anything when it came to solving crimes involving African Americans.

Barry shook his head.

"Detective Roan, we need you to find Jeannine and lock her up in jail or an asylum. I will walk you outside. Thank you for coming."

"Mr. Garrett, if I was you, I would get additional security installed around the house."

"Detective, I plan to do that for the house, our cars, and offices."

"Good. It appears that Jeannine really does have it out for your wife."

"I tried to appear composed in front of Neisha because I did not want to add to her anxiety. However, that deranged woman has invaded our personal space and safety. If necessary, I will hire someone to find her."

"I understand. I will ask my superiors if we can put a few extra officers on assignment to locate Jeannine. I will also request increased police patrol in this area."

"Thanks."

Detective Roan carried the box to his car and securely placed it in a corner of the trunk.

Once inside the car, he made a call from his personal cell phone.

The man on the other end of the phone answered, "Hello."

Detective Roan responded, "Sir, both Neisha and Barry are fine."

"Well done, Roan. Thank you. Continue to check in with me regarding this situation. Make sure that they remain out of harm's way."

"Will do."

Detective Roan hung up.

Inside their home, Barry tried to comfort and reassure Neisha.

"Ne, I am going to call Russell and tell him we need alarm systems installed immediately. I am sure he knows of a company that provides 24-hour service. Perhaps, they can send someone out today."

"Barry, I am not up to that ruckus. Anyway, it is almost time for you to leave. Do not worry about me. I am fine. Those young men at that juvenile camp need you. Jeannine will not be foolish enough to try anything else today. I am tired. All the excitement has worn me out. I'll take a long hot bath, read, and go to sleep."

"Are you sure, Ne? I can reschedule."

She was adamant.

"I am absolutely sure. The devil ain't running anything here. Go ahead. When you come home, maybe we can go out for dinner or something."

"That sounds like a plan."

"Barry, why does that woman hate me so much?"

"It's not you, Neisha. It is her envy of what God has done in your life. Remember that the prodigal son's brother did not rejoice when he returned home. I really do not want to leave you like this."

She rubbed her stomach.

"All is well."

They went upstairs.

Neisha lay on the bed while Barry showered and changed clothing.

Before Barry left, he reaffirmed that she felt safe.

Neisha poured her favorite aromatherapy bath liquid in the tub until the bubbles covered any possible glimpse of water.

As she lay in the tub, Neisha recalled when she realized that she had outgrown her friendship with Jeannine. She had emotionally matured, but it appeared that Jeannine suffered from emotional and spiritual delays. Also, it seemed that forces of death, destruction, and despair were drawn to Jeannine like magnets.

One night, Neisha had a horrible dream that Jeannine harbored a secret that caused her extreme distress. The next day, she telephoned Jeannine and told her about the dream. She offered to lend an ear if Jeannine needed to talk.

Jeannine informed Neisha that she found evidence of Kenneth's adulterous behavior with an older woman, one of her patients. She found letters and pictures in a dresser drawer. Jeannine snapped when she confronted the woman. She pulled a gun on the woman, tied her up, and held her hostage while she searched for more information regarding the affair. When she untied the woman, she threatened to kill her if she told anyone.

Neisha was appalled. She did not validate Jeannine's actions as she may have done in the past.

"Jeannine, you had no right to hold that woman hostage in her own home."

Jeannine became angry with her.

"Neisha, she had no right to violate my marriage. I thought you would take my side. Screw her and you too."

Neisha called in an anonymous referral to Adult Protective Services.

Two weeks later, Jeannine claimed that she found the woman dead of some mysterious food poisoning.

Neisha suspected foul play and that Jeannine might have been involved.

In another incident, Jeannine's daughter, Vanessa, was offered a job out of state as a buyer for a major department store chain. Vanessa gladly accepted the opportunity to obtain gainful employment and move far away from Jeannine.

When Jeannine found out that she was not a part of Vanessa's plans, she had a fit. She accused Vanessa of being ungrateful. She told Vanessa that if she left, she would be sorry.

Vanessa argued back that Jeannine used her to frame Kenneth and eventually abandoned her. Vanessa told Jeannine that she had never been a mother to her, and she did not give a dam about her threats. She informed Jeannine that if she did not stop threatening her, she would tell the authorities that Kenneth never molested her.

A few weeks later, Vanessa almost perished in a fire in the home where she lived with Jeannine. Vanessa was adamant that her mother tried to kill her. She believed that Jeannine had drugged her and set the fire.

According to Vanessa, she felt groggy and went to bed. The smell of smoke awakened her. The house was engulfed in fire and smoke. She attempted to escape when she realized that her keys were not on the dresser where she had left them. Since the front door had a double bolt lock and security bars were nailed to the windows, she ran towards the back door. A piece of burning wood fell from the ceiling and fell on her head. Her face and hair became inflamed. She tried to put the flames out with her nightgown. Fortunately, a firefighter axed through the door and carried her outside.

Vanessa was adamant that she observed Jeannine standing a few feet away, holding Vanessa's keys, and with a sinister smile on her face.

Jeannine did not ride with Vanessa to the hospital.

Vanessa suffered second and third-degree burns to 40 percent of her body. Her beautiful hair was burned to the scalp. Her face required several skin grafts.

The insurance company and police conducted an arson investigation. The cause of the fire was ruled as inconclusive.

Jeannine did not visit Vanessa in the hospital. When Vanessa was released, Jeannine would not allow Vanessa to live with her. Jeannine continued to hold a grudge.

B arry used all the emotion and fervor in the depths of his soul to minister the word of God to the young men at the South L.A. Juvenile Facility. Several accepted salvation.

Barry was pleased that God used him to reach out to others during such a turbulent time in his life.

When Barry returned home, Neisha was sound asleep. Her Bible was open to Psalm 91. He did not awaken her.

Barry focused on getting alarms installed and finding Jeannine.

As he changed clothes, he received a call from a restricted number. Barry went downstairs to prevent Neisha from hearing his conversation.

Neisha's nonprofit organization provided free and sliding scale community and faith-based services to disenfranchised men, women, and children. It is located in an urban part of Los Angeles known as "The Jungle."

The Jungle is a crowded region of apartment buildings that host a high crime rate amongst individuals who primarily live below poverty level. Drug and gang related activities are common. Drive-by shootings occur on a more than occasional basis. Any given day, a resident might walk outside and have to step over a dead body in the parameters of their building. Most police officers of that particular precinct don't usually respond to calls, leaving most citizens to go to the station to file complaints.

The majority of the property owners are slumlords of various ethnicities, races, and religions who accept low-income housing vouchers and were unconcerned about their tenants' safety and well-being.

Neisha's pregnancy created an urgency to make several personnel changes within the organization. She planned to hire someone immediately. Based on her client population, she needed someone who could balance intelligence and diplomacy as well as being street smart.

Over the past few months, Dae remained sober and diligent. Neisha prayed daily that Dae maintained the positive changes in her behavior. As long as Dae maintained her newfound work ethic, Neisha had less to worry about.

Yavette began working with Neisha as a volunteer and was Neisha's first salaried employee. Neisha planned to promote Yavette to a management position, which would leave an opening for an administrative assistant.

Neisha placed ads in several local newspapers and asked friends and associates to spread the word. The response was overwhelming.

Within a week, Neisha received over one hundred resumes. She narrowed the list of qualified candidates to twenty. She immediately scheduled interviews for five of them and prayed that one would be the successful candidate.

After interviewing the first four candidates, Neisha was not impressed. Two were overqualified. One was too arrogant. One declined the position after gaining a better understanding of the population that was served. There was one candidate left to interview after lunch. If the candidate was not appropriate, she would schedule additional interviews.

Before returning to the office and the dreaded forthcoming interview, Neisha stopped by the local office supply store. When she returned to work, she pulled into the parking lot and began removing bags from her car.

An attractive young woman exited the car parked next to Neisha's.

Neisha smiled and said, "Hello."

The young woman barely acknowledged Neisha. She nodded and continued the conversation on her cell phone.

As Neisha eavesdropped, she realized that she was the subject of the conversation.

The woman stated, "Girl, I have to go inside for my interview with 'her holiness." I did my homework. It appears that Mrs. Garrett is a notable figure in the world of ministry and nonprofit organizations. She has one of those "guttermost to the uttermost" testimonies. That is fine with me as long as she does not expect me to fast and pray at work, or walk around saying, 'Praise the Lord and hallelujah' all day."

Apparently, the woman's homework did not include a picture of Neisha. She had no idea that Neisha and "her holiness" were the same person.

The woman walked away and entered the building.

Neisha entered the building from the rear door.

Neisha paged Yavette on the intercom. "What is the name of the next applicant?"

"Sasha Slade."

"Yavette, I will interview her now."

Sasha entered Neisha's office. Her view of Neisha was obstructed by Neisha's large black leather office chair.

Neisha purposely kept the rear of the chair facing Sasha.

"Please have a seat, Ms. Slade."

Neisha provided Sasha enough time to sit down comfortably. Then, she slowly turned the chair around and looked directly at Sasha. She stood up and extended her right hand. She mocked parts of Sasha's phone conversation.

"Praise the Lord and hallelujah. I am her holiness. Oops, I mean Neisha Garrett."

Sasha recognized Neisha as the woman who spoke to her in the parking lot. Aware that Neisha overheard her conversation, Sasha stood up, prepared to leave the office without an interview.

"Mrs. Garrett, I would like to extend my most sincere apology. Sometimes, my mouth gets the best of me. I have been known to suffer from 'stuck my foot in my mouth' disease."

"Sasha, you should get an antidote. By all intents and purposes, I should show you out of my office. Fortunately, for you, I overheard the challenges that you were having with finding employment that accommodates your school schedule. Since I am pro-employment and education, please hand me your application. While I review it, tell me a little about your goals, dreams, aspirations, where you come from, and any other pertinent information. Keep it real. The guttermost in me recognizes game when I hear it."

Amazed, Sasha could not believe that Neisha did not kick her butt out of the office after the way she mad dogged Neisha in the parking lot.

"Mrs. Garrett, do you really want me to keep it real, formal or informal?"

"Ms. Slade, keep it real and informal."

Sasha knew an opportunity when she saw it. She sat down and began to tell her story. At the age of four, her mother asked a neighbor to babysit for a few hours. After three days had passed, and her mother had not returned, the neighbor called Family Services.

Subsequently, Sasha bounced from one foster family to another for the next several years. Her mother bounced in and out of her life like a rubber check. Ms. Anne became Sasha's foster mother when she was in middle school. Ms. Anne provided her with guidance and direction. She helped Sasha foster a sense of hope.

As a sophomore and senior in high school, Sasha worked as a tutor. She received cash and an educational stipend. She enrolled at Cal State University. During her last year in the bachelor's program, it seemed as though all hell broke loose. She exhausted her stipend money, was no longer eligible for assistance from Family Services, and her roommate was behind in her portion of the rent.

Somewhat impressed, Neisha summoned Yavette. "Please give Ms. Slade the employment tests and a trial run on the phone."

Yavette replied, "Sure."

When Sasha finished, Yavette met with Neisha to provide a report. She laid the test results on the desk.

"Neisha, she has potential. She aced everything."

Niesha replied, "Hmmm. I'd like to offer her two weeks of temporary employment. If it goes well, I'll offer her a permanent position if she can pass probation. What do you think?'

"Ne, it sounds good. What will I do if you hire her full-time?"

"You will take over most of my responsibilities. You practically know more about my job than I do. On your way out, please send Sasha back in."

"Humbug," Yavette stated.

Neisha explained her plan to Sasha and asked about her availability.

"Sasha, I know this is last minute on a Friday afternoon, but can you start this Monday at 9:00 a.m.?"

"Yes, ma'am, of course. You will not be disappointed. Thank you so much for taking a chance on me."

"Sasha, please call me Neisha. When you arrive, check in with Yavette."

"Ms. Neisha, I see why God has been so good to you. Have a great weekend. I'll see you on Monday."

Neisha laughed.

"If I don't decide to take the day off.

At approximately 2:45 p.m., Neisha left work. Satisfied that she might have hired a new administrative assistant, Neisha planned to spend some quality time with Barry.

During dinner, Neisha told Barry about her encounter with Sasha.

He laughed.

"Ne, that sounds a little like you back in the day."

"Barry, it was hard as hell for me to stand there and eavesdrop on her conversation without telling her that I was Neisha Garrett. When she came into my office, and I turned that chair around, I thought she would pee on herself. Then she would have had to work as a cleanup woman for free."

"Ne, you are crazy. You two should get along fine."

After dinner, they adjourned to the living room. Neisha put a movie in the DVD player. Barry stretched out on the sofa. He laid his head on Neisha's lap. She massaged his temples.

They were halfway through the movie when Barry kissed the inside of Neisha's thigh.

"Baby, I am more in the mood for acting out our own movie. I can play the lead actor who is making passionate love to his leading lady."

Neisha replied, "Show me what you got, Casanova."

The following morning, Neisha did not remember when she went to bed. She looked over at Barry. He laid on his stomach asleep.

The phone rang. Neisha looked at the clock. It was 7:00 in the morning.

"Hello," Neisha answered.

It was Bettye.

"Neisha, wake up. I have some news to share with you. I am so excited. Sis, I know it is early morning there, but I just couldn't hold the news much longer."

"Bettye, give me a moment to go into the other room. I do not want to wake Barry. He is knocked out."

Neisha walked to the adjacent bedroom. She sat down on the bed.

"Okay, Bettye, why are you so excited?"

"Ne, you know that television network, the one we call "the churchy station.""

"Yes. The one we said would never let any saved hood rats like us on it. What about it?"

"Apparently, on the night of the revival, someone from the station was there as a guest. That person told the station manager about the service. Hold on, Neisha, let me catch my breath."

"Bettye, you better keep talking. I feel like I am hanging off a cliff."

"Ne, the station manager and a producer telephoned David. They requested to meet with us to audition for a show they were considering. We auditioned but had not heard anything. We figured it was a fluke. Anyway, they called today. David and I received the parts. The show will air for 30 minutes,

190

once a week. The target audience is real people, not celebrities, who have been delivered from various addictions and afflictions. Of course, we want you and Barry to appear on the show."

Neisha was astounded. She muffled a shout.

"Oh my God! Hallelujah! Bettye, I am sincerely happy for you and David. The enemy knew that once you broke free from captivity, there would be hell to pay. That is why he kept using yo crazy momma to keep you bound. Look at how God is going to use you as a vessel to help others. I do not know about appearing on the show. I would have to act too dignified to be on the churchy station. They ain't gonna have all that shouting and holy rolling on there. I can't wait until Barry wakes up so I can tell him."

"I know you are happy for us. The station needs a change of venue. Why else would they give David and me a show?"

"Bettye, because you have been set free and you are walking in God's favor. And that station has needed a change for years."

"Yeah, that is true. Anyway, that is enough about us. If Barry is knocked out, he must have had a rough night."

"Yep, he did. What they. say about pregnancy, hormones, and horniness is true."

Bettye laughed.

"How are you hanging in there? I am going to spoil my godchild rotten. I can't wait until he or she is born."

"The morning sickness has mostly subsided, the cravings are crazy, and my hormones are all over the place. You know that I am excited, but a little fearful. I pray that the generational curse is broken. Barry will be a great father. I just wish my baby had some close maternal relatives. Nonetheless, you, Barry, and Momma Flo are not going to spoil my baby. I will do that all by myself."

"You two will make great parents. If the baby is a girl, she will wrap Barry around her finger. You will have some competition. Shoot, boy or girl, that baby will be preaching and laying hands on people by the age of five. Go back to sleep. I love you, sis."

"I love you too, Bettye."

Neisha hung up.

When Neisha entered the master bedroom, Barry remained asleep on his stomach. She climbed into bed next to him. She thought about Bettye's news. "Glory to God," she proclaimed before drifting off to sleep.

It was after 10:00 a.m. when Neisha woke up. She looked over at Barry and laughed. That would teach his dirty old man self to mess with her when she was trying to watch a movie.

After she showered and dressed, Neisha proceeded downstairs. It was nearing lunchtime, so it seemed senseless to cook a large breakfast. She decided that home fries, toast, and eggs would be enough.

The expectant parents planned to look at baby furniture and get ideas on designing the nursery. Neisha knew she should wait until she was further along in her pregnancy, but she could not help herself or at least she did not want to.

B arry entered the kitchen and inventoried the food on the stove. He licked his lips when he saw the home fried potatoes.

"Neisha, honey, what are we having to eat with these home fries?"

"Scrambled eggs and toast. We'll get something else while we are out."

Barry frowned.

"Ah, c'mon, pooh. I haven't eaten since last night. I worked off my dinner making love to my sexy, pregnant wife."

She knew that he was desperate when he called her pooh. She retreated to the refrigerator and took out turkey bacon and biscuits.

Barry stated, "That's my girl. I will treat you to dinner wherever you want to go."

She gave him the hand and rolled her eyes.

Neisha retorted, "It will be dinner time before we leave. Oh, by the way, Bettye called while you were sleeping. She and David are going to have a show on the churchy station."

Shocked, Barry replied, "No way. They will be the first interracial couple to host a show on that network or any of those other religious networks. I know that Bettye is your girl, but she can be ghetto."

Neisha repeated the entire story. She also informed him that they wanted them to be guests on the show.

"Ne, I gotta call David. I'll be in the den."

"Oh no. You can call him after we have finished our errands. Y'all will start talking about work and sports. Breakfast will get cold. Suffice it to say that I will have an attitude."

194

He kissed her forehead.

"Ne, I'll be off the phone by the time breakfast is ready."

Barry swiftly headed towards the den.

Neisha, alone in the kitchen, threw up her arms.

"Lord, I guess I will have to get used to having two babies on my hands."

He kept his promise. Barry was on the phone for a matter of minutes. After he finished his conversation with David, he returned to the kitchen to assist Neisha.

As Barry sat down, he opened his mouth to say something.

Neisha interjected, "So, I guess that you want to go to Atlanta."

"Wifey, sometimes I think that in addition to your other talents and gifts, you are a mind reader. It would be nice, but I have been taking a lot of time off work lately. It may not be safe for you to fly."

She grinned.

"Let's talk about it later. I would love to go. If we cannot fly, maybe we can do one of those video things. Please bless the food so that we can eat."

Barry prayed.

"Father God, thank you for this food. Let this food nourish our bodies and our minds. We pray for those who need spiritual or physical food. We also pray for those who hunger for righteousness. Let their stomachs and spirits be filled. In Jesus' name, Amen."

Neisha repeated, "Amen."

The following Monday, Sasha arrived forty-five minutes early for her trial tour of employment. She sat in the car and read a textbook. To say that she was excited was an understatement. Based on her background, there was not too many people willing to take chances on her in the past. Neisha Garrett was special.

Yavette arrived before anyone else at the office. She waved and waited for Sasha to exit her car.

"Good morning, Yavette."

Yavette smiled.

"Hi Sasha. You look nice. Let's go to my office. I have paperwork for you to complete. When you finish, I will introduce you to the other employees. Some may bark, but they don't bite."

The women entered the building.

On the opposite side of town, Dae waited in the lobby for her appointment with Dr. Lynette Richard, an internationally known expert in the field of HIV and AIDS.

Dae recalled when her primary care physician informed her that she tested positive for HIV. She was devastated. She did not try to comprehend what the doctor said about people living longer who were HIV positive, or that HIV is not necessarily a death sentence.

Dae confronted him.

"Who do you think you are fooling? You have no idea how long I will live. There is no cure for HIV. I am going to die a horrible, painful death."

Immediately after her diagnosis, Dae went on a wild shopping spree and maxed out several credit cards. She figured that if she were going to die, she would die broke. She thought about selling her townhouse and relocating to an apartment in a less expensive area of Los Angeles. Ironically, once she found out that she was HIV positive, her thoughts focused on the child and husband that she might never have.

Dae personalized her disease. She did not know when she became infected. God only knew how many men she transmitted the disease to over the years. Despite her promiscuous behavior, she never practiced safe sex. She wondered if the person who transmitted the disease to her knew that he was positive.

It was a rude awakening, but Dae realized that her vengeful attitude had backfired. Her "love them and leave them" mentality, which she harbored from being abandoned at the altar, may have contributed to her predicament. She recalled that "The Bible" said that vengeance belonged to the Lord. She should have left it in God's hands. Well, as her granny had said, "there is no fool like an educated one."

After reviewing Dae's lab results, Dr. Richards commended her.

"Dae, keep up the good work, which probably means that you have made positive lifestyle changes. I presume that you have quit or curtailed partying, sexing, and drinking. Are you working on developing extended support from friends and family?

Dae broke down in tears. "I have burned so many bridges. I am working on making amends. For the most part, it seems as though it is just God and me."

After she spoke the words, truth and validity slapped her in the face. She realized that nothing mattered except establishing a new and foundational relationship with God. After all, God was able to do abundantly and exceedingly above all things. With His help, she could learn to live with HIV. She could also reunify with her family of origin as well as Bettye and Neisha. Hell, she might even find a man who would accept her with her infirmity.

That night, Dae sought God's full attention. She sat at her desk in the study and read her Bible. In the midst of reading, she began to pray and cry. Dae fell on her knees, lay prostrate, worshipped, and asked God for forgiveness. The prodigal daughter and chronic backslider repented.

The next morning, Dae attended 6:00 a.m. prayer. She did not focus on anything other than her reasons for being there. She prayed that God would change her heart, heal her, and help her work through her bitterness. She left the church feeling refreshed and renewed. It was time to clear the air with Neisha.

Things were going well at the office. Sasha had been employed as administrative assistant for several weeks. She was a blessing in disguise. Yavette maintained her dependability. Dae had been sober for a while.

Neisha and Dae were alone in Neisha's office to discuss work related business. Neisha gave the other employees the remainder of the day off.

"Neisha, before we get started, I have something important to tell you. You know I am working a 12-step program and trying to be open and honest."

Neisha frowned. "Dae, I feel some sort of confession or amends connected to that statement."

"Neisha, I am HIV positive."

Neisha tried to remain calm. Her mind immediately flashed back to when Dae tried to seduce Barry.

"Dae, did I hear you correctly? I am not judging your choices or lifestyle. But was there a possibility that you could have infected Barry if he had been gullible or stupid enough to sleep with you?"

"Neisha, I don't think I had HIV at that time. Please hear me out. You are my best friend. I know that I seldom act as though I appreciate you. I am sorry for all the hurt that I have caused you. We all make mistakes. We signed a pact."

"That was the same pact that existed when you tried to sleep with my husband, backstabbed me on several occasions, and all the other countless and vicious things you have done to me throughout the years. For the most part, I ignored or forgave you. I should fire your ass right now. Not because you have HIV, but your arrogance could have put my husband's life and mine in jeopardy if he was stupid enough to succumb to temptation."

"Neisha, have a heart. You are a Christian. I need my job and my insurance. Most importantly, I need a friend."

"Dae, don't even try to use the Christian hold card on me. I am so sick of people trying to play guilt on folks when they think it is to their benefit. Get out of my office and my life!"

Neisha felt dizzy. She grabbed her stomach. She grimaced in pain. She lay back in the chair, motionless and with her eyes closed.

Dae ran to the employee lounge, opened the white metal door of the first aid kit, and removed the smelling salts. She returned to where Neisha remained motionless in the chair. She bent down, placed the smelling salts under Neisha's nose.

Dae frantically yelled, "Neisha, wake up."

After what seemed like an eternity, but was only a few moments, Neisha woke up. She felt weak.

She whispered, "Dae, please call Dr. Webster. I do not feel well. I have cramps.

Dae telephoned Dr. Webster's office. Kim instructed Dae to drive Neisha to the emergency room at Central Hospital. Dr. Webster would meet them there.

Dae helped Neisha on one of the office chairs and wheeled her to the car. S

She prayed, "Lord, please let Neisha and the baby be okay."

At Central Hospital, Dr. Webster and two orderlies waited outside the emergency entrance door for Dae and Neisha's arrival.

Dae drove the car to the front of the hospital emergency door entrance and swiftly opened the passenger's door.

The orderlies rushed to the car and lifted Neisha onto the gurney.

Neisha looked at Dr. Webster.

"Doc, save my baby."

He nodded.

Neisha whispered to Dae.

"Please call Barry."

Dae responded, "I will as soon as they get you inside."

Neisha reached into her purse and handed Dae her driver's license and medical card.

Dae entered the reception area and gave Neisha's information to the triage nurse.

Introducing Malik

A fitting description of Bishop Malik Anthony Tolbert is fine. In acronym format, the letters would imply that F is for Fine, I is for Intelligent, N is for Not Married, and E is for Extremely Well Off Financially. Physically, he is a cross between NBA greats Michael Jordan, Rick Fox, and Reggie Theus. He is six feet, two inches tall and muscularly ripped. He does not have a six-pack. Malik has a twelve pack of muscles all extenuated in the right places. His unblemished complexion is a deep dark, chocolate cocoa brown. When he smiles, he reveals a deep dimple in his left cheek. His mother use to say that an angel kissed him there when he was born. His lips are sensuous and sexy. Malik's hazel colored eyes often change colors depending on his wardrobe.

Malik's father currently pastors the largest church in Dallas, Texas. His mother is the first lady. He has six brothers and two sisters. The entire family is involved in some form of ministry. Malik is a third generation pastor.

During his senior year of high school, several NBA scouts attempted to recruit him. He was fortuitous enough to realize that there is no immediate guarantee to fame and fortune. He pursued a college degree and majored in Theology.

After graduation, Malik signed with a professional basketball team in southern California. During his first two years on the team, they won back-to-back championships.

During Malik's fifth year with the team, he severely injured his left leg in a car accident. As a result, most of the cartilage and bones in his leg were replaced with pins and metal. His pro basketball career was finished. Fortunately, he had a college degree and an astute manager who invested his funds wisely.

Toi, Malik's beautiful wife, was an uppity gold-digger. Although she earned large digits annually as an agent for high profile athletes, she spent Malik's money as if it was water. On the surface, they appeared to be a glamorous, wealthy celebrity type couple. That was purely superficial. Toi also looked down on the other players' wives, primarily because they were content with being housewives. On several occasions when Malik returned home after a long road trip, she refused to make love to him. After his injury, Toi filed for a divorce. She had no desire to be a preacher's wife. After the divorce was final, she married a professional football player.

Malik pastors a huge nondenominational church in Inglewood, California. It has a Pentecostal foundation but is not a holiness church. He has approximately 15,000 documented members. A large percentage of members and visitors are middle to upper class African American yuppies, celebrities, lawyers, doctors, and athletes. The church takes in millions of dollars a year in tithes, offerings, grants, and donations. The church has approximately one hundred salaried employees and a countless number of volunteers.

Several African American publications have featured Malik as one of the most eligible and wealthy bachelors in the U.S.

Malik's two-story, five bedrooms home sits on a hilltop in the Baldwin Hills area of Los Angeles. The home casts an electrified view of the city. An oval-shaped, deluxe Olympic pool monopolizes the backyard.

Malik and Barry became acquainted at a fundraising event. After a lengthy discussion, Malik and Barry realized that they had several mutual interests. Their friendship developed from there.

B arry needed to vent. He invited Malik to lunch at Rudy's, an upscale restaurant located on Restaurant Row in Beverly Hills.

As Malik sat in the booth awaiting Barry's arrival, he sipped on raspberry iced tea and scanned his appointment book.

When Barry arrived, the concierge escorted him to the booth. Barry gave Malik a high five and sat opposite him. The conversation began with catching up on the latest in sports before Barry changed the subject.

Barry stated, "Man, I invited you to lunch is because I need to do some male bonding. I am excited about the baby and all, but Neisha is driving me crazy with her cravings and mood swings. She is a strong woman, and I am not used to her whimpering."

Malik laughed.

"You'll be okay. Remember your wedding vows. You promised to love her both in sickness and in health."

At that moment, two equally attractive women walked in the direction of Malik and Barry. They passed their phone numbers to the men.

Barry shook his head and held up his ring finger.

Malik laughed it off.

Barry commented, "Malik, those were two bold women."

Malik seized the opportunity to vent his frustration.

"Barry, what is wrong with these aggressive, immoral, and unscrupulous women? I have requested that additional male workers occupy the front pews near the pulpit of my church. Some women sit in the front pews, cross their legs, and display all their family jewels. Others stand up, bend over, and display their thongs. If this is the type of behavior that some display in church, I can only imagine how they behave in the community. I have lost count of how many so-called saved, holy, and sanctified sisters have tried to approach me with some kind of proposal. Some are young, old, single, married, White, Black, Hispanic, or Asian. A few of them are married to deacons and elders. Temptation is consistently present."

Malik paused for a moment, sipped his beverage, and continued speaking.

"Man, I am ready to settle down. I welcome the idea of getting married and having a sanctified, real woman of God like Neisha. The majority of my church will not be receptive to any woman I bring in as my first lady. The numbers may plummet but so be it. I would trade happiness and the sanctification of marriage for membership in a moment. Electric blankets and cold showers grow old and tiring after a while. You are a lucky man, my friend. What you are going through is temporary. Look at the long-term benefits of your legacy and love. Count your blessings."

"Malik, you seem to have it all. I never realized that you were so lonely. You are right, I am truly blessed. My wife and I love each other. We are expecting our first child. What we are experiencing is temporary."

Barry changed the subject.

"Do you remember Neisha's friend, Jeannine Clark? Her daughter was burned in a fire."

"I remember the daughter. She often attended affairs with you and Neisha. I do not recall her mother."

Barry told Malik the complete sordid affair, including the threats, the police involvement, and the package left at the front door.

Malik responded, "Man, what you described sounds like one of those black movie dramas made for television. What are you going to do? Let me rephrase that. Do not do anything that you may regret later. Remember that God has brought you from a mighty long way."

"Malik, I don't know what I will do."

The waitress brought their food to the table. She bent over and purposely exposed the cleavage of her bosom as she placed their plates in front of them. The short, flared skirt flew up an inch or two and exposed more thigh. She smiled, unashamed and flirtatiously. As she walked away, she added an extra dip in her hips.

Malik laughed.

"Man, do you see what I mean when I say there is way too much temptation?"

B arry barely finished eating his prime rib dinner when his cell phone rang. The caller ID displayed Dae's name. He wondered why she would be calling him. He answered in a flat, unfriendly tone.

"What is it Dae?"

Dae's voice quivered. "Barry, meet us at Central Hospital. Neisha is in the emergency room. She fainted. She is having cramps and bleeding a little. Dr. Webster is here. I gotta go."

Dae hung up before Barry could interrogate her.

Barry stared at the phone.

"Malik, that was Dae. Neisha is in the emergency room at the hospital. I have to leave immediately."

Malik exclaimed, "Oh my God! Let's go, I'll drive. We will return for your car."

Barry paid the tab.

Malik owned an impressive collection of late model and antique cars. He drove to the restaurant in his silver Jaguar XJE sedan with tinted windows.

As the two men fastened their seat belts, Malik paused.

"Barry, let's pray before we leave."

Barry nodded.

Malik prayed.

"Father God, please protect us as we travel. I bind any assignment and attack of the enemy against Barry and Neisha. We declare and decree that Neisha and the baby are out of harm's way. We ask that you place a hedge of protection around this family. No weapon formed against them will prosper. We submit this petition in the name of our Lord and Savior Jesus Christ. Amen."

Central Hospital bordered the cross streets of Olympic Boulevard and Crenshaw Avenue, an approximate thirty minute ride from the restaurant.

Malik drove safely and swiftly on the surface streets. He did not know what to say to console his friend, so he kept silent.

Barry sat in the gray leather seat facing the tinted passenger window, lost in thought. He was grateful that passer buyers could not see the tears streaming down his face.

Malik brought the car to an almost screeching halt in front of the entrance to the emergency room.

Barry exited the car and rushed hurriedly through the automatic glass sliding doors. He noticed Dae seated in the waiting room reading a magazine. He approached her.

Dae looked at him, apprehensively.

"I was not permitted to go in with Neisha. Dr. Webster is examining her now."

Barry glowered at her. A hint of his Belizean dialect surfaced. The tone of his voice was just above a whisper, and he spoke rapidly. He did not wish to cause a scene, but he wanted answers.

"Dae did you have anything to do with this? I better not find out anything that remotely connects you with endangering Neisha and our child."

Dae shook her head.

"No, Barry, I did not."

Barry proceeded towards the nurse seated behind the triage window.

"Ma'am, my name is Barry Garrett. I would like to see my wife, Neisha.

"Mr. Garrett, the doctor is examining her. I will let you know when he is finished. It is against hospital policy for me to interrupt."

"I understand. Thank you."

Barry sat down. He felt helpless. He looked towards the door and wondered what was delaying Malik.

Malik realized that his behavior had been somewhat erratic over the past few months. He sat in his car to reevaluate things. He needed to appear cool, calm, and collected when he entered the hospital. He would tease Dae and tell her how good-looking she was, as he often did. He would display any type of façade necessary to hide the truth, which was becoming increasingly difficult to subdue.

Malik was in love with Neisha. However, reality had just hit him like an 18-wheeler. Neisha and Barry were expecting a baby. Someone appeared intent on harming Neisha. The two events strengthened the bond between Barry and Neisha. Malik was certain that his love or lust for Neisha blocked his desire to date or be involved with other women. He faithfully repented whenever the feelings began to overwhelm him.

He telephoned the chief of his security staff, Benji Hale, from his cell phone.

Benji answered, "Hello."

Malik inquired, "Benji, how are you?"

"Good, Malik."

"I have an urgent, personal matter that needs investigation. I need information concerning a woman named Jeannine Clark immediately. Be discreet and collaborate with a minimal number of people whom you trust explicitly. I will place you on retainer. Name your price."

"Malik, I'll make it a top priority. We will talk about money later."

"Thanks, Benji. Goodbye."

When Malik called, Benji Hale was home watching the NBA playoffs. He could not believe that Houston scored a basket in the final 10 seconds of game six. The score was 99 to 97. The Lakers lost by one lousy basket. That cost him fifteen hundred dollars. The sportscaster added insult to injury by repeatedly showing replays of the game.

Benji grabbed the remote, pushed the red power button, and turned off the t.v.

Benji's boxers and t-shirt were soaked with perspiration. The distinct smell of marijuana and cocaine filled the den. Benji stumped out the tip of a primo joint in the ashtray.

Malik would fire him if he knew about his issues with gambling and marijuana. Benji laughed at the irony. It appeared that Malik needed security to monitor his chief of security.

Between sips of his ice-cold brew, Benji tried to remember why the name Jeannine Clark stuck in his memory. Several moments later, it clicked. Her name was associated with a terrible relationship that he longed to forget.

When he was deep in the world, totally unsaved and amoral, he worked at a nightclub as a bouncer. Jeannine Clark frequented the club regularly. She was not the hoochy type. She dressed conservatively, and her demeanor was reserved.

Bennie recalled that Jeannine often remained at the club until nearly everyone else had left. After a few months had passed, she invited him to breakfast after work. He accepted. They dated. He pointedly told her that he was not interested in a monogamous relationship with one woman. She

215

claimed that she was okay with that. Jeannine periodically spent the night at his place.

As time passed by, he realized that she was whack. She became controlling and manipulative. If he left her alone in his car or apartment, she rambled through his belongings. When she located women's phone numbers, she called and cursed them out. She jeopardized several of his business ventures and friendships. When he confronted her, she played the victim and blamed her behavior on loving him. He would feel sorry for her. They sexed and made up.

After several months, he was done, and he broke up with her. A few days later, someone keyed his car, left scratch marks on it, and put sugar in the gas tank.

Less than a week later, Benji arrived home from work around 3:00 a.m. The outdoor lights were off. The place was dark. Since the lights were on a timer, he feared that someone might have burglarized his home. With his flashlight in one hand and gun in the other, he entered. When he flipped the light switch in the living room, the room remained pitch dark. Instinct led him to check the stove. There was no gas. He turned on the hot water faucet. The water was ice cold. When he picked up the phone receiver, there was no dial tone. Defeated, Benji drove to a motel.

At the motel, Benji telephoned the emergency services at the utility companies. Each representative gave the same report that his wife had placed an order for the service to be disconnected. He explained that he was single and lived alone. He demanded that his service be restored immediately.

To avoid any further interruptions, he requested a password for his accounts. In the future, no changes or cancellations were to be made without the password.

There was no doubt in Benji's mind that the woman who falsely represented herself as his wife was Jeannine. He called her and informed her that he never wanted to be bothered with her ever again in life. He threatened to get a restraining order against her.

Benji's mind went forward to the present. He was astounded. Why did Malik want information about Jeannine? Anything associated with Jeannine had to be trouble. Malik could not afford a scandal. Benji also could not fathom any mutual associations between Malik and Jeannine.

Bingo! Benji recalled that Jeannine had a friend named Neisha. He realized she was Barry's wife. Malik's request was associated with Neisha.

Benji shouted in the air.

"Payback is a mutha, Jeannine. I'm gonna get paid to get back at you."

Grinning from ear to ear, he went into the kitchen and retrieved a cold brew from the fridge.

Perspiration tainted Benji's underwear and emitted a funky odor that even he could not stand. He stank. He stripped off his shorts and t-shirt and threw the items in the brown wicker clothes hamper. While he showered, he sang and plotted revenge against Jeannine.

Benji dried his body with a huge bath towel. He grabbed his navy blue velour bathrobe and slipped on the matching slippers. He sat on the side of his bed and telephoned Terrance Freeman.

Terrance was a lieutenant in the highest ranking black mafia organization in Los Angeles. He kept tabs on everything that might impact the organization and the city, whether it was legit or illegitimate.

When Terrance heard Benji's voice, he immediately asked, "Man, you got muh money?"

"No, I don't have your money, but I got a new gig. I need information, but I cannot talk on the phone. Can you meet me at "The Spot" tomorrow evening around 6:00?"

"Yeah, man, but you better have a good plan about how you gonna get me muh dam money."

An associate of Jeannine's, who worked for a healthcare agency, owed Jeannine a huge favor. After Jeannine escaped from the institution, she blackmailed the woman into getting her a live-in caregiver position. So far, no one had traced her whereabouts.

Alone in her room, she was having a psychotic episode. She felt frantic and extremely paranoid. Her plans had soured. Originally, she wanted to place a little fear in Neisha. Somehow, things got out of control. Now the police, and only God knew who else, were probably looking for her.

Jeannine did not have friends or family to ask for help. She could not call her psychiatrist, as he might surrender her to the police or lock her up. She was determined not to return to an insane asylum. As she had done in the past, she began to plot and scheme as to whom she could manipulate to help her.

Jeannine recalled that her ex-lover, Benji, worked for that big-time preacher, Malik Tolbert. She would get Benji to help her.

Jeannine removed her stationery kit from the desk. She began writing a note to Benji.

In the meantime, Doc Webster accompanied by a nurse, continued his examination of Neisha.

He scolded, "Neisha Garrett, I told you to take it easy."

"Doc, I have been taking it easy. But there has been a lot of stressful stuff going on in my life lately."

He motioned for her to put her feet in the stirrups.

"Please relax. Now, show me where you are experiencing the most pain."

Neisha pointed to the lower middle section of her stomach.

Doc Webster gently touched the left and right quadrants of her abdomen.

She grimaced in pain. "Ouch!"

"Neisha, how long have you experienced this discomfort?"

Neisha twisted her face, still in pain.

"Uh, for a few days."

He shook his head and completed the examination. He dismissed the nurse.

"Neisha, you had a close call, but you and the baby are fine. Based on your history of miscarriages, I am very concerned. You need to rest and remain off your feet for a few days. I know if you return home, you will not comply with those conditions. Therefore, my recommendation is that you remain in the hospital for the next 48 to 72 hours."

"Doc, I cannot possibly stay in the hospital for the next two or three days. I must take care of my husband, and I have a business to run. Please release me and do not talk to Barry. I promise to take better care of myself."

Doc Webster did not bite.

"I am sure Barry can take care of himself. Where is he? Maybe he can talk some sense into you. You need to set your priorities straight."

At that time, a nurse interrupted them.

"Doctor, Mrs. Garrett's husband is very impatiently waiting in the lobby."

"Thank you. Please send him in."

The nurse returned to the triage area and summoned Barry.

"Mr. Garrett, please enter when you hear the buzzer."

Barry wrung his hands nervously. He put his sweaty palm on the door handle and opened it.

The nurse instructed him to go to bed number 17.

Barry entered through the open curtain on the left side of Neisha's bed. He kissed her on the forehead.

She extended her arms, seeking comfort. She stated, "Hi Barry, Doc Webster says the baby and I are fine."

Barry sought confirmation from Dr. Webster. "Doc, is that correct?"

"Yes, Barry, at least for now. I strongly recommend that Neisha remain in the hospital for two to three days."

Neisha attempted to voice her objections.

Barry firmly stated, "Neisha Lynette Fuller-Garrett, it is not open for discussion.

Neisha looked defeated. She gave Barry her pouty look.

Barry ignored her.

"Doc, she will follow your orders and recommendations. Admit her immediately."

Doc Webster felt a little sorry for her.

"Is that right, Neisha?"

"Yes, tattletale."

Doc Webster replied, "It is for your own good."

Neisha nodded.

Doc Webster excused himself to arrange Neisha's admission.

Once Barry established that no one was within hearing range, he confronted Neisha.

"What is wrong with you? Are you crazy? Do you want this baby?"

"Of course, I do! How dare you insinuate otherwise?"

"Well, you need to get it together. When Dae called, I feared the worst. You and I have discussed that superwoman mentality of yours. It is time to take that "S" off your chest, hang up your cape and costume, and place them on the shelf. You are not the only one under a lot of pressure. If anything happens to you or that baby because of your neglectful attitude, we will revisit whether or not we should remain married."

Neisha was shocked. Barry never threatened to leave or divorce her. He really was pissed.

She started to cry.

"I'm a bundle of nerves and hormones. Who is going to take care of you and the business while I am here?"

Barry rubbed his right temple as he often did when he was frustrated. He hated it when she cried.

"Ne, don't cry. Everything will work out. Dae and Yavette can fill in for you at work for the next few days. We will discuss things further when I return. We must have faith. I have to leave. Malik has to drive me to the restaurant to retrieve my car. I will go home and pack a bag for you. You know that I love you, but sometimes you can be so damn hardheaded and stubborn."

Suddenly, Neisha felt an odd pain in her right side like a kick. It felt like something knotted up inside of her. She bent over slightly. Her face twisted and her eyes bulged. Excited, she grabbed Barry's hand and placed it on her stomach. It was the first time the baby moved.

"Barry, the baby kicked. I can really feel life growing inside of me. I am going to be a mother."

He looked at her as though she were having a "duh" moment. As his hand lay on her stomach, there was a distinct and forceful movement underneath.

Barry shared Neisha's enthusiasm. "Ne, with a kick like that, it must be a boy."

Neisha smiled.

"I don't care about the sex of the child as long as he or she is healthy."

Barry gently let go of Neisha's hand.

"I will ask Dae to remain at the hospital until I return. Then, I will stay until they tell me to leave."

"Okay, Barry, I would like that."

He kissed her gently on the lips and left.

Barry located Dae and Malik seated in a corner of the waiting room. He approached them. "Everything is fine for now. Neisha will have to remain in the hospital for a few days. I would like to thank each of you for having our backs."

Malik sensed that his friend was still worried.

"Barry, where is your faith? During times like this, you have to place your trust in God!"

"Yeah Malik. Man, it seems like it is one storm after another. It is as if we are in a hurricane season of trials and tribulation. What else can I do but trust God?"

Barry turned his attention to Dae.

"Will you please stay with Neisha until I take care of a few errands? Just don't let her get worked up about anything."

"Sure Barry. First, I need to call Bettye. If she found out that Neisha was in the hospital and I did not let her know, she would be pissed, to say the least."

"Thanks, Dae."

Barry turned to Malik.

"Let's go."

Dae went outside and telephoned Bettye. She could not recall the last time that she called Bettye for anything. She had isolated herself in her misery.

When the phone rang, Bettye recognized Dae's number on the Caller ID. She answered, "Hello Dae, how are you?"

Dae sobbed hysterically after she heard Bettye's voice.

"Neisha is in the hospital. She nearly miscarried. Barry is distraught. I need you to pray for them. I am also facing health challenges. Please pray for me as well."

Bettye shouted, "Oh my God, are Neisha and Barry okay? Is Neisha having any problems with the pregnancy? I'll be on the next plane that I can catch coming to LA."

Dae responded, "Bettye, that's not necessary. Barry is hanging in there. It looks like Neisha will be in the hospital for the next few days. Let us wait and see what happens."

"Dae, promise that you will call me or have Barry call me if anything changes. As we both know, sometimes Neisha is too stubborn to ask for help."

"Bettye, I promise."

"Dae, what is going on with your health?"

"I would rather not talk about it yet. Can we pray now?"

Betty prayed.

When they finished praying, Dae stated, "Thanks so much. I need to check on Neisha. I know I don't say it often enough, but I love you."

Dae did not wait for a response. She hung up.

Bettye plopped down on the sofa before she fell down from the shock. How sick was Dae? What was going on with Neisha? Was it something brought on by Jeannine? What in the world was happening on the other side of the country?

She walked upstairs and packed a suitcase in the event that she needed to travel to Cali in a hurry.

Malik dropped Barry off at Rudy's. Barry reached in his wallet and gave the parking stub to the valet. After the valet retrieved his car, Barry tipped him and drove off.

Barry entered the home and went upstairs to the master bedroom. His eyes gleaned the bed that he would sleep in, alone, for the next few nights. He was mad as hell. Why was God letting them go through this? He pounded a pillow several times with his fist. Barry felt extremely powerless.

"Father God, why is this happening? I know that Neisha and I have not always lived a godly life. I have hurt some people really bad. According to your word, you forgave me for my sins. Lord, I am putting my trust in you. Help us, watch over us, encamp your angels around us, and place a hedge of protection around my family. Please do not let anything happen to Neisha and the baby. Don't punish them for something that I may have done. Oh God, strengthen me in Jesus' name."

A tear rolled down Barry's right cheek. He removed one of Neisha's overnight bags from the closet. He grabbed undergarments, nightgowns, and hygiene items and placed them in the bag. He went downstairs, secured the alarm, and left.

Neisha lay in the hospital bed and stared at the sterile looking curtains that separated her from the other patients. She wanted to go home. But she knew that the most important thing was to do whatever was necessary for the health and safety of her and her baby.

She wondered if she would not be in this dilemma if Dae not told her she was HIV positive. However, she realized that it was not Dae's fault. It was a buildup of stress and overextending herself. Barry was correct. It was time to put her "S" on the shelf. She was not a super shero. She had to initiate serious lifestyle changes.

A nurse came to the curtain. "Mrs. Garrett, are you awake?"

Neisha answered, "Yes."

"An orderly will be here shortly to take you upstairs to room 8127."

"Thank you. My friend, Dae Gordon is in the lobby. Can you please tell her that I am fine and ask her to bring me something to eat?"

"Sure Mrs. Garrett. There are no dietary restrictions in your chart."

Neisha thanked her.

Dae entered Neisha's hospital room. She washed her hands and gave the food to Neisha.

Neisha calmly stated, "Thanks Dae, I am too tired to rehash what happened at the office. I promise that I will not disclose the information about your medical condition to anyone, not even Barry. As your employer, I can't. You can remain on the job. But let me make myself quite clear. If you ever cross my husband or me again, we are finished as friends and business associates, pact or no pact."

Dae hugged Neisha.

"Ne, I know being my friend has not been easy."

"Dae, that's an understatement."

While Neisha ate, they reviewed the impending plans for the office over the next few days.

Barry entered the room.

Dae knew that was her cue to leave.

"Neisha, I have to be going. I will check on you tomorrow. Bye, Barry, Neisha."

Barry replied, "Thanks, Dae, we appreciate all that you have done."

Dae left.

Russell Demetrius Jones was born and raised in Compton, California. He had two brothers, one older and one younger.

As a child, Russell liked school, especially sports. He did not do well academically. He deplored science and math. His parents constantly scolded and reprimanded him about his grades. They compared him to his older brother, Paul. They felt that investing in Russell was "a waste of time."

In the 10th grade, Russell began ditching school. He hung out with an incorrigible crowd that always seemed to get in trouble. He smoked weed and took downers.

When Russell was 18 years old, he was busted for joyriding. It was his third offense. He did not steal cars. He just liked to ride. The judge gave him the option of going to jail or serving in the war. Russell chose the latter. He felt that since he was from Compton, the army would not faze him.

Russell enlisted in the United States Army. After boot camp, he was deployed to Vietnam. He soon learned that gangbanging in Compton was nothing compared to the war in Vietnam. Russell used drugs to cope.

The U.S troops massacred entire families, including children. The Vietnamese fought back with a vengeance. On one occasion, a young girl, around the age of 10, ran out of a hut ready to blow Russell's brains out. She had a gun in her hand with her finger on the trigger. He killed her in self-defense. Many of his friends were murdered, maimed, or taken captive and held prisoners in POW camps.

Russell returned home as a decorated war hero. He received a Purple Heart for courageous acts against the enemy. However, his heart felt numb, and his spirit was dead. No medal of honor would fix his mental, spiritual, and emotional anguish. He often remembered the mines blowing up. Sometimes, it felt as if explosions set off in his head. He would never be the same.

Russell moved in with his mother and father. His sanctified parents called him a "baby killer." They said that he broke the worst of the "Ten Commandments." They told him that because he committed murder, he would never gain entrance to heaven. They treated him with worse indifference than they did before he fought for his country.

Despite it all, he remembered the commandment, "Honor thy mother and father." He would not reciprocate their emotional and verbal abuse. He left their home.

Russell moved in with his younger brother, De'Andre, who was heavily involved in drug dealing and gang activity. His brother was big on the set and balling out of control, a real shot caller. Russell sold drugs for De'Andre to keep a roof over his head and support his drug habit.

Russell often worried that his brother would go to jail for a long stretch or die in one of the current territorial gang wars. His worries were valid.

De Andre's so-called friend, Junebug, set him up with rival drug dealers. De'Andre was killed during a drug deal that went bad. Even in the devil's handiwork, one should expect the unexpected. The people whom Junebug plotted with against

De'Andre killed him as well. They assumed that if Junebug turned against De'Andre he could not be trusted.

Since law enforcement and Internal Revenue did not place liens on De'Andre's property, his parents inherited everything that De'Andre owned.

Russell's parents were not too holy to accept ill-gotten gains. The so-called saints also kept the "tainted drug money" in De Andre's bank accounts and safes as well as his cars, jewelry, and other expensive items. They even drove the cars, with tinted windows and gangster rims, to church.

Russell's parents blamed him for De'Andre's death. They did not allow him to remain in De'Andre's home and rented it out. Wherever Russell could find a place to lay his head became his shelter. He often wandered the streets and frequented places where addicts and alcoholics congregated.

Russell felt consumed by depression, fear, and hopelessness. He often hallucinated and became delusional.

A physician at the Veterans Administration Outpatient Clinic diagnosed Russell with Post-Traumatic Stress Disorder. Russell was placed on a regimen of psychotic medications. He hated the side effects and self-medicated with drugs and alcohol.

Russell and Barry became acquainted at one of the places where Barry sold drugs. Barry would give him drugs when he was short. Barry would also send him on errands or give him tasks to help him out. Despite Russell's addiction and erratic behavior, Barry looked out for Russell.

When Barry got busted and went to the penitentiary, Russell enrolled in a drug treatment program for homeless veterans. He successfully completed the program within a year. He met a lawyer who helped him file for a service-connected pension. His pension and back pay were approved. Subsequently, he and Barry became partners in a limousine business and other legit ventures.

Russell remained estranged from his mother and father.

Russell's father was diagnosed with prostate cancer. His saintly mother placed her husband in a convalescent home. She did not have time to care for a disabled person. She was too busy travelling to conventions and flossing at church. When he was in hospice, she went to a church convention. He died while she was out of state.

T he day after Neisha was admitted to the hospital, Barry went to her office to deal with a few items that required attention. Russell accompanied him. He went into the lounge to wait.

Dae was seated at a table, eating a salad and reading a magazine. She looked up when she heard Russell's footsteps.

Russell spoke first.

"Excuse me. I didn't know anyone was here. I'll leave if you want to be alone."

Dae responded, "Russell, please stay. I could use the company."

Russell sat in the chair next to her.

"Dae, how is life treating you? I have not seen you since Marie's funeral."

"Russell, things are okay. It could be worse."

"Yes, Dae, they could be. As long as you woke up this morning and are above ground, things will work out. Have faith."

"Russell, that's ironic. I was just thinking about going to visit my granny. She used to say almost the same thing.

Dae and Russell talked for over half an hour. She could not recall when she enjoyed the company of the opposite sex in a purely platonic fashion.

Russell invited Dae out for a date.

"I have two orchestra seat tickets to a play in Hollywood. It stars the guy who plays that crazy old woman. Would you like to go out to dinner and the play?"

"Sure, Russell. Here's my number."

The Spot was an underground men's social club inconspicuously located in the heart of midtown Los Angeles. The upstairs attic was converted to a small brothel for exclusive clientele. Services were available by appointment only. Gambling was offered a few nights during the week. Security was tight. The owner of the club had politicians and police on the payroll.

When Benji arrived at The Spot, Terrance was shooting pool. Benji approached him.

Terrance motioned for the other person to leave. He racked up a new set of balls and handed Benji a pool stick.

"Benji, where is muh money?"

"Terrance, I will get your money real soon."

Terrance frowned.

"Fool, I give you one week to come up with five grand. How are you gonna work with a broken arm or leg? Maybe I will call that high phalooting preacher that you work for and tell him to give me muh money."

Benji carefully strategized how he would bust open the balls on the table. He stretched out his right arm and took a shot. Four balls landed in various pockets.

"Terrance, I told you that I would get your damn money. I got a new gig. For now, I need to know the word on the street about a woman named Jeannine Clark."

Terrance slammed the pool stick on the table. The remainder of the balls went everywhere. A few landed on the floor.

"Shut up and follow me. Don't say another word."

Benji was frightened by Terrance's unexpected reaction. He followed Terrance to a room with three double bolt locks. Terrance unlocked the door. After he entered, he summoned Benji to come in.

"Sit down."

Benji stammered. "Whaaat the hell is the matter?

Terrance looked Benji eye to eye.

"You can't repeat what I am about to tell you. Someone wants that woman found really badly. I heard over 50g's bounty, dead or alive."

Benji could not believe what he heard.

"All right, I am on it. You will have your money next week."

"Okay, Benji, I better. I'll walk you out. No gambling for you today."

After he left "The Spot", Benji called Malik and told him that he may have a lead concerning Jeannine. He needed money as soon as possible. The men agreed on $10,000 as a retainer for Benji's services.

Benji knew that Jeannine was crazy. He still could not believe that there was a bounty on her head, and the illustrious Bishop Tolbert sought information about her.

Benji resolved to locate her. As he recalled, she had a daughter and an ex-husband. Then, he remembered that Vanessa, Neisha's so-called niece, was Jeannine's daughter. He laughed out loud. Things were falling in order too well.

Terrance retreated back to his office and securely locked the door. He grinned. He told that fool Benji that the bounty was $50,000 when it was actually $100,000. Terrance reached for the phone and began dialing.

A man answered.

"Yeah, what's up?"

Terrance replied, "Boss, you ain't gonna believe this. A square just came by asking about old girl. He said that he has been hired to find her."

"You don't say." Did you give him any information?"

"Just enough to make him run outta here like his pants were on fire."

"Hmm, our friend needs to be kept close. Let him think that he has had a run of good luck. Help him out at the tables. Do not have anyone follow him. He will get the information for us.

"Bro, I got it covered. That fool still better pay me muh money."

The man on the other end of the phone laughed before he hung up.

On the other side of the country in Atlanta, David's and Bettye's show was a tremendous success.

After Neisha was released from the hospital, they interviewed Barry and Neisha in Los Angeles. The show had the highest rating that the network ever received.

Behind the scenes, a young, attractive White camerawoman named Suzy flirted with David.

It soon became evident to quite a few people that Suzy favored working with David in opposition to Bettye.

Faye, Suzy's co-worker and friend, confronted her.

"Suzy, why are you shamelessly flirting with David?"

Suzy played coy. In her southern accent she asked, "Faye, what do you mean?"

"You are always in his face. You treat his wife like crap."

"Faye, he is a sexy, attractive White man. What is he doing with that Black spade?"

"I can't believe that you said that! Obviously, neither of them is in it for the money. They both have their own. You need to remember that she is in front of the camera and your White ass is behind it."

Disgusted, Faye walked away.

Bettye is not a person to mask her feelings or observations. She invited Suzy to lunch.

After they ordered beverages, Bettye opened the discussion.

"Suzy, I invited you to lunch to discuss why it appears to me that you have your eyes set on more than just viewing my husband through your camera lenses."

"Well, Bettye, since you are so candid about your feelings, I may as well be honest. I am attracted to David."

Betty laughed.

"Well, let me get a few things straight with you. You are not the first young White, Brown, or Black hussy who has tried to sleep with my husband. You may as well step down off your high horse for several reasons. First, once you go black, you don't go back. Second, David is not into the kiddy playground. He plays at Bettye's World, the grandest of amusement parks. Third, I sincerely doubt that you can beat me rocking, so I am not worried about you taking my chair.

Suzy turned scarlet red. She grabbed her purse.

"I won't be staying for lunch. I didn't really want to eat with a nigger in public anyway, especially since I am not working."

"Suzy, I'll talk to the producers. If I get my way, you won't be working with this nigger or her husband any longer."

Suzy stormed off.

Bettye summoned the waiter and ordered lunch. While she waited, Bettye called Neisha and told her what happened with Suzy.

"Bettye, watch yourself. You know the wrath of those southern White folks. Didn't you watch 'Roots'?"

"Yes, I watched it, but I don't plan on losing a leg or anything else. I don't trust Little Ms. Thang one bit. I am sure this is not the end of it. Why don't people leave me alone? Now, I have to put up my guard for her and Janice.

"I know what you mean. Remember the struggle is real, but God has our backs," Neisha stated.

"Ne, maybe that is why folks are always hating on us. My food is here. Talk to you soon."

"Bettye, be careful. I will be praying for you."

"I love you, Ne."

Bettye hung up.

Dae and Russell began dating regularly. People were shocked. The two were literally as different as night and day. Russell appeared to bring the best out in Dae. He treated her like a lady, not an object. She treated him with respect. Dae could handle Russell's periodic episodes of PTSD.   Russell accepted Dae's HIV positive status.

Dae did not have any complaints. Her health was stable. Work was fine with the exception of the new employee, Sasha. They were a lot alike, almost carbon copies. Sasha had mouth, but she was sharp. She was also loyal as hell to Neisha. She got on Dae's nerves.

Dae decided it would be a suitable time to visit her parents and her Granny.

As Dae exited the plane, she took a deep breath. She had not returned to the city since her wedding fiasco. Facing family and acquaintances would not be easy.

Dae hailed a cab. Inside the vehicle, she rolled down the window. The brisk, chilly air smacked her face with a vengeance. While she stared out the window, she realized that not much had changed along the scenic route visible from the freeway.

Granny waited outside for Dae's arrival. She sat in the rocking chair on the porch. She was ecstatic that Dae decided to be a guest at her house.

Dae and Granny spend a lot of time together. They went shopping, to the movies, and had a wonderful time. Dae's mother, Gladys, accompanied them on a few occasions. Dae did not contact her siblings, any of her old friends, or associates.

One evening, Dae disclosed to Granny that she was HIV positive. She waited several moments for her grandmother to respond.

Granny was shocked.

"Dae, I thought only drug addicts and gay men got HIV. Do you use drugs?"

"No, I got HIV from having unprotected sex with supposedly heterosexual men."

Tears formed in her grandmother's eyes.

"Dae, did you come home because you are dying?"

"Granny, we all are going to die someday. I am doing fine. I am on medications. I have made several lifestyle changes. I watch what I eat, exercise, pray, and I don't sleep around. As a matter of fact, I am celibate."

"Well, that's a relief. Are you going to tell your parents?"

"Yes."

"They will have a fit, especially your father. You know that you have my support."

Dae cried. She wiped at the tears.

"I know, Granny."

On Sunday, Dae attended church with her parents and Granny. Afterwards, they ate dinner at her parents' home. After dessert, Dae broke the news to her family.

"Mom and Dad, I have something to tell you. I have been ill. I have HIV."

Gladys' hand grasped the left side of her chest as if she were going to have a heart attack.

Leroy called Dae every vulgar name he could spit out of his mouth. He was furious.

"You used our dishes and sat on our furniture. I hope your trifling ass didn't infect us with anything. Get out of my home, you slut or dopehead, whatever you are! Only faggots, whores, and drug addicts get that disease."

"Father, as usual, you are being ignorant. HIV is not contagious, so do not go throwing away dishes and furniture. I'm not a dopehead. I did not make the wisest decisions in having unprotected sex with men."

For once, Gladys showed some courage, some heart. Usually the passive housewife, she intervened on Dae's behalf.

"Leroy, shut up. How dare you talk to this child like that? You have always demanded perfection from her. Whenever she fell short, you rejected her. You will not do it this time. She needs us."

Gladys rose from her seat, tears falling down her face, and hugged Dae.

"You do not have to go anywhere."

Dae cried as well.

"Thanks, mother, but this place has never felt like a home to me. As soon as I could get out, I did. I slept around looking for love or something to fill a void."

Leroy yelled, "Don't try to blame us for you catching some disease because you were a whore."

Leroy jumped up from the table. He went into the living room and grabbed his jacket and keys.

As he stormed out the door, he yelled, "Screw both of you."

When he exited, he slammed the door with so much force that the room shook.

Dae kissed Gladys on the cheek.

"I love you, mother. My flight leaves in a few hours. I have to get ready. We'll talk soon."

Dae and Granny said goodbye to Gladys and left the home.

A short time later, Dae heard a knock at the door. She looked through the peephole. It was Gladys. Dae opened the door.

Gladys held an envelope in her right hand.

"Dae, I have something for you. Somehow, now seems like the right time to give it to you. Maybe, it holds some answers for you."

It was a letter. Dae stared at the envelope. The handwriting belonged to Mark.

"Mom, this was from Mark. It is dated a few days after he abandoned me at the altar."

"I know Dae, and I am sorry."

Dae's taxi arrived. She kissed her mother and grandmother.

Granny stated, "Dae," if you need anything, please call me. I love you."

"I love you too, Granny."

Gladys yelled, "I love you. I'll call you soon."

During the flight, Dae opened the letter from Mark Roberts.

My Dearest Dae:

I apologize for abandoning you. I truly do love you.

When I received the results of my blood tests, I was HIV positive. I am sure that I transmitted the disease to you. I did not know what to do, and I could not face you. I took the coward's way out. Please do not hate me.

As you know by now, I have left my job and apartment. I've relocated to another state.

Please forgive me.

Love Always,
Mark

Dae could not believe it. She may have been infected with HIV for years. She wanted a drink. She needed Russell. She quietly cried herself to sleep.

When she arrived at the airport, Russell was there to greet her.

As they got in Russell's car, Dae stated, "I want to spend the night at your place."

Russell asked, "Are you absolutely sure?"

Dae nodded.

Russell smiled.

"I'll stop by a store and purchase condoms."

Dae smiled. She kissed Russell on the cheek and placed her hand on his knee.

As Benji left work one day, he was approached by a homeless man that lived on the streets in close proximity to the church. The man had an envelope in his left hand.

"Hey isn't your name Benji?"

Benji asked, "Why?"

"Some chick gave me $20 to hand you this envelope."

"What did she look like?"

"Man, I can't really say. She wore dark glasses and a big hat. She drove up and called me to the car. She said that she knew that you worked for Bishop Tolbert. She gave me the money and told me to give you the letter."

"Thanks. Are you sure that she did not say anything else?"

"No, she handed me the letter and the money and hightailed it out of here."

Benji began to walk away.

The man yelled, "Bro, are you gonna grease my palms with something?"

Benji gave the man $20. He walked to his car.

The man ran away.

Benji opened the envelope. He immediately recognized Jeannine's handwriting. A one page note was enclosed.

Hello Benji:
It's been much too long. I am in deep trouble. I need your help.
Please meet me at the Cameo All Night Theater on Los Angeles and 7th Street at 2:30 a.m. on Wednesday morning. There are no cameras so there will be no history of our meeting. I'll be sitting on the right side of the theater, fourth row from the door.

Regards,
JC

Early Wednesday morning, Benji parked several blocks away from the Cameo All Night Theater. The theater was part of the 90013 zip code that included downtown skid row.

Benji was skeptical about parking near the theater as he did not want Jeannine to see what type of car he drove. However, he concluded that if Jeannine had been spying on him at work that she could probably identify his car.

A few stars twinkled in dark sky a distance from the full moon that provided light above. As he walked towards the theater, Benji observed homeless people asleep in alleys, doorways, and on sidewalks. Cardboard boxes and tents cluttered pathways. Men and women pushed shopping carts as they searched for recyclables. Others were dealing or smoking drugs, tweaking, or trying to obtain a basic need such as food, sleep, safety, or shelter.

After Benji paid admission, he entered the theater and walked towards the rows of chairs on the far right. He observed a woman sitting in the fourth row from the rear. She occupied the chair near the wall. A blanket covered the woman's head.

Benji walked towards the woman.

She whispered, "Psst, Benji, it's me."

Benji sat next to the woman.

"Jeannine?"

"Yes."

Jeannine disclosed how she escaped from the mental institution. She further disclosed how she harassed Neisha and threatened to harm her.

Benji asked, "What the hell do you want me to do?"

Jeannine answered, "I need you to help me make this thing with Neisha right. I can survive these streets as long as I know that none of her folks are out to get me."

"Jeannine, why should I help you?"

"Because if you don't, I'll go to your employer with some information that I've obtained since I came home. It seems like you spend lots of money on drugs and gambling. I also have some old news about you that I can use for my current benefit."

Benji shook his head. "Same old Jeannine. That's why your ass is in trouble now. "

Jeannine and Benji met in remote places where it would be difficult to link them together at any given point.

Jeannine usually talked about making amends with her daughter, Vanessa, and Neisha. She was under the illusion that once she resolved her issues with Neisha that she could go underground and still have ties to a worldly existence.

Benji pretended not to know much about Neisha other than what he occasionally read in the papers about her outreach efforts and community involvement. He convinced Jeannine that he would need money to pay his contacts and get information.

They took advantage of each other. They were master manipulators and opportunists.

Neisha had cravings for lasagna. She made reservations for lunch at a popular Italian restaurant in Hollywood.

Following her doctor's appointment, Neisha took a taxi to Barry's office.

As they prepared to leave, his phone rang. Barry answered and was extremely abrupt and rude to the person on the other end of the phone. It became obvious that he did not want to have a conversation in Neisha's presence.

Barry whispered, "I am taking my wife to lunch. Yes, that is correct. We will discuss the matter later. I am sure I will not require your assistance."

Visibly irritated, Barry hung up.

Neisha eyed him suspiciously.

"Barry, who in the world was that on the phone?"

"Sweetheart it's nothing for you to worry about."

Barry walked around the desk, helped her out of the chair, and attempted to kiss her.

She turned away.

During the ride to the restaurant, Barry made attempts at conversation. Neisha ignored him.

At the restaurant, Neisha remained aloft. She fumbled at her food with her fork. Finally, she broke her silence. With tears in her eyes, she whispered and quite candidly asked, "Barry, are you having an affair?"

Barry was flabbergasted.

"Neisha, you know me better than that. You know I love you with all my heart and soul. You are more than a handful. I could not possibly manage an affair mentally, physically or spiritually. I am no fool. I know what I have at home. There is no way I would give up filet mignon and settle for ground beef. I have always honored our marriage vows and will continue to do so. We are in this until death do us part."

"Barry Lamont Garrett, I am tired of you treating me like a child or some delicate, fragile piece of China. I am an adult. Most importantly, I am your wife. Quit hiding things from me. I hate secrets!"

Barry did not respond.

During their meal, the tension between them was so thick that it could have been cut with a knife. They hardly spoke to each other. After they completed their meal, Barry drove Neisha home. He returned to his office.

He knew that Neisha was furious with him, but he could not tell her that somehow Carlos had found out about their problems with Jeannine. Most importantly, he could not tell her that Carlos wanted to help them solve their troubles.

That evening, Barry and Neisha remained civil through dinner.

Afterwards, Barry put the dishes in the dishwasher. Neisha went upstairs to the nursery. She sat in the mahogany rocking chair and rocked back and forth.

At the beginning of their marriage, Barry and Neisha promised that they would never go to bed angry at each other. Yet, Neisha remained angry from the day's earlier events. She was not going to sleep in the same bed with him. He would sleep on the sofa or in the guest bedroom. He could sleep with his secrets.

Neisha was at the end of her wits, confused. The two of them were not secretive in the past. She could not understand what was happening to them. She thought their marriage was based on a solid foundation. Now that she was pregnant, she desperately wanted her child to have something that she lacked, two loving parents and a home.

She closed her eyes. Her mind drifted. She thought about separating from Barry for a while. Suddenly, she felt a tap on her shoulder.

"Ne let's talk.

She ignored him.

He asked, "Do you want to get up or do you want me to carry you?"

He offered his hand and helped her from the chair. They walked into the master bedroom and sat on the bed.

Neisha knew his history of employment with Carlos. During his last jail term, he could have turned informant and given Carlos over to the police and the

258

feds, but he did not. When Barry was released, Carlos rewarded him for his loyalty. Carlos helped Barry invest in the limo business with Russell. He left the organization with Carlos' blessings. As far as Barry was concerned, the debt was settled.

"Ne, I was talking to Carlos on the phone, not another woman. Someone is leaking our business to him. For the life of me, I can't fathom why. He keeps calling me and asking me questions about our safety and well-being. You know that everything I do nowadays is legal and legit."

"Barry, I believe you. Why would this man care about what happens to us now?"

"Ne, for the life of me, I do not know."

They discussed Momma Flo's proposed relocation. They would help her obtain a place pending the sale of her home, or she and Deidre could stay with them for an abbreviated time. They agreed that they needed her help immediately.

Early the next morning, Barry phoned his mother.

"Hello mom, how are you?"

"Hello son, me good. How be you, Neisha, and me soon to be grandbaby? Something must be lurking if you call me dis early in de morning and be calling me 'mom'."

"The truth is that the water is a little troubled. We have some problems. I was wondering when you can move out here. We desperately need your help."

"What be you talking about boy by asking me when? De house is on de market for sale. All me need to know where me and Deidre can stay. She be out da school next week. Me have gotten rid of much stuff. We packed what we needed to bring with us. De rest, you will hire a truck for transport and pay for de storage."

"Of course, you and Deidre will stay with us. We have room. Let me know about the truck. I can't emphasize how much we need you."

Barry paused for a few seconds. When he resumed speaking, his voice trembled.

"Mother, I cannot lose my wife or baby. I just cannot."

"Boy, rebuke the devil, and him flee. We bind him foolishness in the name of de good Lord. Put Neisha on speaker. We pray right now."

When they finished praying, Momma Flo provided further words of encouragement.

"We will be in Los Angeles a few days after Deidre is out of school. If need be, we come before. Just hold on my children. Jesus loves you and so do I. Goodbye."

A few weeks after Barry's frantic call, Momma Flo and Deidre relocated to Los Angeles. They moved in with Barry and Neisha. Momma Flo was ecstatic.

Neisha loved Momma Flo, but she drove her crazy. Every morning when Neisha woke up, Momma Flo made sure that Neisha rubbed her stomach with cocoa butter so she would not get stretch marks. She prayed with Neisha.

On the other hand, Momma Flo helped with cooking and cleaning. She monitored Neisha's food intake. She rebuked the thought of a housekeeper or stranger in the home.

Deidre was a blessing. She learned to drive. Barry bought her a car and she acted as chauffeur/gopher for Neisha and Momma Flo.

Despite it all, Neisha loved the idea of having family around.

On the other hand, Barry felt like he would lose his mind being the sole male living with those females and their hormones. Although, he had to admit that he relished the attention he received. They all doted on him. He realized that he had better enjoy it. Once the baby arrived, he would no longer be the center of attention.

Barry's hormones were out of sync. He yearned to make passionate love to his wife. Dr. Webster recommended that they refrain from lovemaking for the last 6-8 weeks of Neisha's pregnancy. He was certain the increase in the water bill was largely due to an increase of the cold showers he took. There was some consolation in knowing the journey was almost over.

B enji and Jeannine went to remote places to be together. He could not risk being seen with her in public. She could not risk someone recognizing her.

One particular morning, while they lay in bed, Benji thought about how he had gotten caught up in such a mess. He derived a sense of pleasure when he thought about the financial gain at the end of the escapade.

Jeannine turned over towards him.

"Good morning, Benji. I'm tired of all this sneaking around between us. I need to find a way to resolve this issue with Neisha. I won't call and harass her anymore. I am going to call her and apologize."

Benji was shocked. He thought, "She has got to be kidding."

"Jeannine, sweetheart, we have to think of a way to fix this mess that won't cause you to be locked up. This is not just about Neisha. Remember that you assaulted someone, and he had to go to the hospital."

Jeannine exclaimed, "I am not going to jail or back to that institution with those crazy people!"

Benji sighed.

"Give me a week to try to come up with a plan. Promise me."

Jeannine lay her head on Benji's chest. "Okay."

Benji felt nauseated and disgusted. He could not stand the sight or smell of her. He cringed when she touched him.

Benji had another issue to resolve. It appeared that Jeannine's daughter, Vanessa, could have been conceived around the time that he and Jeannine were in a relationship. Each time that he brought up the subject, she shut down.

He decided to get a DNA test. He became upset whenever he thought about the possibility that crazed Jeannine may have been responsible for almost killing their daughter.

As Vanessa walked home from the store, a man on a bicycle pushed her to the ground, snatched her purse, and sped away.

Frightened, she rushed home and immediately telephoned Neisha.

"Auntie, I was robbed!"

"Oh my God. Vanessa, are you okay?"

"Yes, it was probably some random thing."

"Call the police station to file a report. I'll call Russell. I'll pay to have your locks changed and have an alarm system put in."

"Auntie, I appreciate getting the locks changed. I don't think I need an alarm system or anything like that."

"I do not want to frighten you, but we do not know where your mother is. Nothing like this has happened before. Someone will contact you within a few hours about the locks and alarms. I repeat, make sure that you file a police report. Keep me posted. I love you."

"You are right about that. Thanks Auntie Ne."

Neisha hung up.

Meanwhile, Benji concluded a meeting with the man who stole Vanessa's purse.

Benji had Vanessa's hairbrush, comb, and lipstick. He hoped that DNA would determine if he was Vanessa's father. He took the items to a lab where a trusted friend worked as a technician. He needed answers.

When Benji arrived home, he rolled a blunt and got a brew out of the refrigerator. He sat on the couch and stared at the blank television screen.

What would he do if Vanessa were his daughter? How would he introduce himself into her life, especially if something happened to Jeannine?

The DNA paternity test results indicated that the likelihood of Benji being Vanessa's biological father was 99.9 percent.

Benji was furious. He could not believe that trifling ass Jeannine kept him estranged from his daughter. Even worse, it appeared that she might have been responsible for Vanessa's near-death experience.

Benji decided that it was time to collect his reward immediately. Jeannine's crazy ass impacted too many people's lives with devastating results.

Later that day, Benji plotted to get rid of Jeannine. He also figured out how he would collect the bounty from Terrance and the additional money that Malik promised him if he located Jeannine.

Benji set up a rendezvous with Jeannine. After they settled on a time and place, he contacted Malik and Terrance.

Several things happened on August 29, 2005.

Hurricane Katrina landed and ravaged the gulf with a vengeance. The impact of the hurricane in New Orleans was devastating. Levees broke, and the escaping waters flooded the city. Buildings were ripped from their structural foundations. People climbed out of the windows to find refuge on the rooftops. High waves of water engulfed automobiles, making them look like toy cars, as they flooded through muddy waters.

Benji was aboard a flight to Jamaica.

Jeannine waited for Benji at the designated motel where they planned to meet, unaware that someone sat outside and stalked her for a change.

Neisha was admitted to Central Hospital in Los Angeles. She and Barry were in the delivery room. Her contractions were less than a minute apart.

Barry commanded, "Push, Neisha!"

"Shut up, Barry. If it were not for you, I would not be in all this pain. This is your fault, you nasty man. Do not ever touch me again. Oooh!"

"Ne, take deep breaths and push. C'mon baby, you are almost there. Remember the Lamaze classes."

"Nothing was trying to tear my insides apart in the Lamaze classes."

Barry shook his head.

"Oh my God, help me," Neisha screamed.

Dr. Webster coached her as well. "Neisha, push hard, the baby's head is coming through."

Neisha felt like she had to make a large poop. She pushed with all her might.

Dr. Webster insisted, "One more big push, Neisha."

Barry saw the crown of a head coming through the vaginal canal. Excited, he yelled, "Ne, baby, you did it!"

Barry and Neisha anxiously waited to determine if their baby was a boy or a girl. Barry Lamont Garrett, Junior was born at 9:35 a.m. on August 29, 2005. Barry was ecstatic, his first son. After the umbilical cord was severed, the nurse approached to take the baby away.

Neisha continued to complain of severe pain. She told Dr Webster that she felt as though she were still in labor.

Dr. Webster examined her. He advised Neisha and Barry to remain in their positions.

Dr. Webster spoke excitedly, "This explains everything. Neisha, you have another baby coming."

Neisha screamed again as Barry's eyes bulged.

Dr. Webster commanded, "Push, Neisha!"

Barry shrieked, "Push, baby, push! I see another head."

Six minutes and thirty seconds later, Jenna Flomarie Garrett, the paternal twin of Barry Lamont Garrett, Junior was born. The triplet, Sarah Rebekkah Garrett, was stillborn, an umbilical cord wrapped around her neck.

Barry and Neisha cried.

Neisha looked at her husband and stated through tear-filled eyes, "We will rejoice. God is good. We have two beautiful babies. Hallelujah."

Dr. Webster shook his head.

"I cannot explain it. The sonogram never showed three embryos or fetuses. There was always one heartbeat. Yet, there was always that veil, that unexplainable covering. I just don't understand it." He scratched the crown of his bald head.

Neisha looked at a seemingly worried Dr. Webster. Her voice was weak.

"Don't worry, doc. It was beyond your control. We will mourn the loss of our beautiful daughter but rejoice for our beautiful babies. One baby is for Barry to tend to during the night, and the other one for Momma Flo and Deidre. I have to recuperate from the past nine months. Now, Dr. Webster, what about some medication?"

He nodded.

The inside of the motel room was dark and quiet. Jeannine heard a knock at the door. She assumed it was Benji.

Jeannine slightly opened the door.

The person on the other side forced the door open. Before Jeannine could scream, the person pointed a gun, with a silencer attached to it, in Jeannine's direction. The bullet blazed forth. And went through her chest cavity and landed in the middle of her heart.

Jeannine fell back on the floor. Blood dribbled from her mouth. Her eyes were wide open.

The next morning, the maid opened the door. She screamed hysterically. She ran to the manager's office. The call to 911 reported that a woman had been murdered.

Detective Roan was the first officer on the scene.

Meanwhile, Momma Flo and Deidre sat impatiently in the waiting room for Neisha to deliver the baby.

An emergency newsbreak pre-empted the regular television broadcast. Hurricane Katrina had ravaged New Orleans. The news anchors covered the devastation from helicopters. News coverage showed people on rooftops, trying to avoid getting swept away in the flooding waters. Buildings, animals, and cars drifted away like toys on a gameboard.

Momma Flo was devastated. She exclaimed, "Deidre, me told you that we had to leave New Orleans. When the good Lord tells you to move, you don't ask questions!"

Momma Flo cried uncontrollably.

Deidre sobbed lightly and lay her head on Momma Flo's shoulder.

After Barry cleaned up and was assured that Neisha and the babies were recovering well, he entered the waiting room.

Momma Flo had calmed down. She stared at the television and rocked back and forth. When she saw Barry, she pointed towards the screen.

Barry watched as the news anchor reported that the death toll was expected to be high. A multitude of people were missing.

In addition to the disaster in New Orleans, Barry had to tell his mother about the baby who was delivered stillborn. He sat next to Momma Flo.

He whispered, "Mom, Neisha gave birth to triplets, two girls and a boy. One of the girls did not make it. The other two babies are in the pediatric care unit. They are doing well. Neisha is sedated. With all this going on, I think the best thing for us to do now is to go home, try to eat, and get some rest."

Momma Flo stated firmly, "Me no go nowhere till me see me grandbabies."

Barry hugged her.

"C'mon, mom. The babies are holding on. Neisha is sound asleep. There is nothing that we can do here. We need to call back home to New Orleans."

Momma Flo thought about her family and friends in New Orleans. "Okay, after me peek at me grandbabies, and then we go.

EPILOGUE

Several days later, Barry, Neisha, Dae, Bettye, Deidre, Momma Flo, Yavette, David, and Russell stood on the grounds of the cemetery by the tiny grave for Sarah's interment.

Tears rolled down Neisha's cheeks as she stared at the tiny casket. Barry held her tight. He cried as well.

As everyone proceeded towards their cars, a handsome, middle-aged African American man approached Neisha. He stopped a few feet in front of her.

"Hello Neisha, how are you?"

Neisha wiped her eyes. Perplexed, she stared at him and asked, "Charles, daddy, is that you?"

"Yes, it's me."

Barry yelled, "What kind of shit is this? Neisha, I know this man as Carlos."

Barry knocked the man out cold with one punch.

Yavette ran to the man, Carlos, aka Charles, and tried to revive him. She shouted, "Daddy, wake up!"

Neisha could not believe what she had just witnessed. She looked over at Yavette as she tried to revive the man. She realized that Yavette must be one of her long-lost stepsisters. Yavette must have been one of the individuals who leaked information to Carlos.

Neisha fainted.

274

Y'all did not see that ending coming, lol!

Things to think about:

- Who was the mysterious man on the phone?
- Is Jeannine really dead?
- Will Momma Flo and Doc Webster get together?
- Will Benji live to tell Vanessa that he is her father?
- Who is responsible for Jeannine's murder, if she is dead?
- Will Susie seek revenge against Bettye?

Stay tuned for the sequel.
Thank you for your support.

ABOUT THE AUTHOR

I am a native of Los Angeles, CA, where I currently reside. I have always wanted to write a book/novel. I hope this novel sets the stage for many more. I aim to excel in writing across various genres. More than that, I hope others are inspired and motivated.

My sobriety anniversary date is 3/27/97 – one day, hour, minute, or second at a time. To God be the glory. In addition to being clean and sober, I have overcome toxic relationships and domestic violence.

After my only maternal, biological sister died, God spoke to me and said *that cemeteries were full of more than bones. Cemeteries are full of dreams and talents that were never realized.* I decided that my hard work would not perish on my laptop. I finally got the courage to self-publish it in my late 60s.

DO NOT GIVE UP ON YOUR DREAMS!

I would love to hear from you:
Instagram: _virgowriter
Facebook: Saints, Ain'ts, and Sistahs-The Novel
           by Toni J. Walker

TONI J. WALKER

SAINTS. AIN'TS, AND SISTAHS

www.ingramcontent.com/pod-product-compliance
Lightning Source LLC
Chambersburg PA
CBHW070847250626
47159CB00003B/976